Perfect Blend: Kofi's Omega

A Bear's Cove Novel

by

A·J· Stone

Bear's Cove 3: Perfect Blend (Kofi's Omega)
Copyright © April 2018 by A.J. Stone
Print ISBN: 978-1-942414-57-5

Editor: Nicoline Tiernan
Cover Artist: Anne Kay

Published by Lost Goddess Publishing LLC

This book is a work of fiction. While reference might be made to actual historical events or existing locations, the names, characters, places and incidents are either the product of the author's imagination or are used fictitiously, and any resemblance to actual persons, living or dead, business establishments, events, or locales is entirely coincidental.

Warning: This book contains sexually explicit scenes and adult language and may be considered offensive to some readers. It is not meant for underage readers.

Building a new life after a failed marriage isn't easy.

Hoyt Graziano is determined to open a coffee shop in Bear's Cove. It's the perfect small town for his shop, Perfect Blend. Only it's also the town where his ex-husband lives.

Lusting after his brother's husband drove Kofi Freeman away years ago.

Now that they're divorced, he allows himself an afternoon of bliss with the man who stars in every one of his fantasies.

But his loyalty to his family makes him reject the vulnerable omega afterward. It doesn't take Kofi long to realize that he made a terrible mistake, but Hoyt isn't impressed with his apology. He's not willing to forgive and forget.

How can he prove his love to a prideful and stubborn omega whose heart he didn't mean to break?

Prologue—Hoyt

"You're wearing that?" Grian wrinkled his nose.

Hoyt Graziano looked down at his outfit of jeans and a blue plaid button-down shirt. This was as dressy as he liked to get, though he knew his father would prefer if he wore dress pants and a tie. "It's a meet-and-greet in a café, not a date."

Grian sighed, while Hoyt's dad, Isaiah, ran a hand through his gray hair. "Hoyt, your father means that you want to put your best foot forward. Make a good first impression."

"I know what he meant. I'm saying that this isn't a big deal. You shouldn't even be there. It'll just make it more awkward. It should just be him and me, sipping coffee and eating biscotti while we ask each other dumb questions."

Arranged marriages were normal among the bears in Forrest Hills and in many other bear communities. From the time he was a cub, Hoyt had expected that his marriage to an alpha would be arranged. His fathers had spent a lot of time cultivating an association with the Freemans, a prominent local family that had four alpha sons to marry off.

Hoyt appreciated everything his fathers did to make sure he had a good life, but he was ambivalent about meeting Dak Freeman. After all, they might hate each other, in which case, the tentative betrothal would fall through.

He glanced over at his fathers. Grian sat in his favorite chair, and Isaiah perched on the sofa with his hand on Grian's shoulder. His parents' marriage had been arranged, and they loved one another deeply. Hoyt wanted that with his life partner.

With a sigh, he got up. "I'll change."

"Wear your red tie," Isaiah said. "The one with the little golden anchors. It brings out the red in your hair."

The red in his hair had never required an accessory to be noticeable. It was the first thing anyone saw when they looked at him. Then they noted the freckles and moved on. A few looked past those long enough to see that his eyes were crystal blue. Though he worked with what he had, Hoyt didn't consider himself a winner in the looks department, but his vivacious and friendly personality often won people over.

The café bustled with people. Hoyt was nervous, and the rich scent of coffee brewing permeated the area. This favorite smell calmed his anxious nerves. People streamed out of the establishment with their purchases and onto the sidewalk where tables and chairs were set out so they could enjoy the sunny day. As the Grazianos stood near the door, searching the crowd for the Freemans, Hoyt peered through the window.

His gaze zeroed in on a man with black hair and blue eyes. His square jaw hinted at a vast well of inner strength, and his sharp cheekbones emphasized the handsomeness of his face. He had broad shoulders and a presence that could not be ignored.

This was the man his fathers had described, and Dak Freeman was so much more than Hoyt had dared dream possible. Dak looked up, and their gazes locked together. Chemistry sizzled, and an invisible line tugged the omega in him closer, reeling him in like a fish on a hook.

"Oh, Daddy." He meant it in an alpha-omega sense. His fathers had said Dak was his age, but this guy seemed a few years older. He was sexy, and he had an air of authority about him that made Hoyt want to crawl into his lap and never look back.

"What?" Isaiah had heard Hoyt's utterance.

Heat traveled up his neck. He hadn't meant to get his dad's attention, but he also didn't want to explain what he'd meant. He pointed through the window. "Is that him? With great enthusiasm, I say yes."

Grian's gaze followed the path Hoyt indicated. His eyes lit. "That's them.

He led Hoyt and Isaiah through the throng and to a place where tables had been pushed together. He stuck out his hand to an older gentleman sitting a few seats from the man of his dreams. "Abe, it's nice to see you. I'd like to introduce my son, Hoyt Graziano."

Abe Freeman rose. He shook hands with Grian. "Good to see you." Then he greeted Hoyt. "It's wonderful to finally meet you. I'd like you to meet my son, Dak." He motioned to a young man seated to his immediate left.

That guy stood. He had black hair and blue eyes, and he bore a strong resemblance to the alpha seated two tables away. He flashed a nervous smile. "Hi, Hoyt. It's nice to meet you."

Hoyt's gaze was pulled to the other man. He turned his head to find those deep blue eyes on him. They spoke to him, called to a primal part of his nature, but rather than continue, they dismissed him, sidling away to stare out the window.

The rejection both stung and felt like a punch to the stomach. His inner bear whined for an alpha who wasn't his intended and who didn't seem interested. With no other option, he forced himself to shake hands with Dak, the man his parents had chosen for him. They knew what was best for him. They knew what they were doing. He had to believe that.

Chapter 1—Hoyt

If marrying the wrong man made for a regrettable start to adult life, what kind of mistake was it for a man to move to the same town his ex had moved to?

And was it worse if the man wanted to open up a business in that town, sort of start over in the same place his ex had started over?

Hoyt thought about that as he considered the piece of real estate surrounding him. He chewed his bottom lip.

The idea to open a coffee shop wasn't a bad idea. Bear's Cove had three, but they could use one closer to the waterfront. He could sell sandwiches and pastries or whatever struck his fancy. This lease space had room on the east side for patio dining, where bear shifters could dare seagulls to mess with them while they ate.

Coffee shops were natural meeting places. They brought people together for all types of events, from friends meeting for a quick cup to business people planning their next big deal to two bears seeing each other for the first time—organically, not the arranged kind of meeting.

While he could have refused the match all those years ago, he had gone through with it from a sense of obligation to his family and his community. So had his ex. Hoyt wanted to make it possible for bears to meet compatible mates and have fun while doing it.

That's why the working title for his new business was Grind-N-Growl.

Bear's Cove was a perfect city, perched on the edge of the sea but still nestled away on hills and surrounded by forests. Hoyt had never considered moving there until he'd visited on that fateful day six months ago when nobody in his ex-husband's family could find his ex to tell him that his fathers had passed away.

Hoyt couldn't turn down that call. He wasn't heartless. Divorce didn't mean he'd stopped caring for Dak, only that he'd finally admitted they weren't in love. Their joining had lacked passion and joy. Sometimes there had been enthusiasm, but that was mostly when Hoyt closed his eyes and pretended he was fucking someone else. Likely Dak had done the same thing.

Hoyt wanted passion and joy. Dak, his ex-husband, had found those things with his new husband, Chase. The only bit of jealousy or resentment Hoyt harbored was that he'd been unable to also find those things. It wasn't fair. He'd left Dak so they could both find happiness. He'd gone off to look for love, and Dak had moved to Bear's Cove to be a deputy. Dak hadn't even been looking for the love that had fallen into his lap. Lucky bastard.

Hoyt had searched through most of the protected lands where bear shifters roamed, but nowhere he visited seemed quite right. The moment he'd stepped foot into Bear's Cove, he felt like he'd found the place where he belonged.

Chase was on board with Hoyt's business plan, especially once Hoyt mentioned opening a coffee shop. Hoyt liked Chase. They were both omegas, and perhaps under other circumstances, the two would have forged a close friendship. What they had now was polite and a little awkward. Hoyt wished it wasn't. Chase had given birth to Ezra, the cutest baby in the world, a few months ago, and Hoyt wanted to spoil the infant in a way only a favored uncle could. Except he wasn't an uncle.

Ulysses, the real estate agent with an ambitious name, grinned. "It's already set up with a commercial kitchen. You won't have to make many changes."

With a sigh, he peered out the windows fronting the store. "Get me the contract on this one so I can read it." Not being an expert on real estate or lease contracts, he wanted to have someone he trusted look them over before he made a commitment. Even if he couldn't get anyone to do him the favor of reading the contracts and giving their opinion, at the very least, he wanted to look everything over on his own.

"I'll send it to your email address." Ulysses tapped away on his phone. "If you have any questions, feel free to ask me. That's what you're paying me for."

While he trusted Ulysses, there was someone Hoyt trusted more. After viewing several more potential sites, Hoyt retired to his hotel room on the outskirts of town. He showered and dressed in comfortable pajamas bottoms, and then he sat on the bed and stared at his phone.

An eternity passed before then he pressed the button to make the call. Kofi Freeman was his ex-brother-in-law and the man he'd originally thought he was slated to marry. The pair hadn't spoken since Hoyt attended the funeral for the Freemans' fathers half a year ago.

Six years older than either Hoyt or Dak, Kofi had rarely been around. Almost as soon as Hoyt and Dak's engagement had been announced, Kofi had bowed to wanderlust. He'd stayed in the area long enough to attend the engagement party, and he'd returned for the wedding. Other than that, he spent the vast majority of his time globetrotting, returning to Forrest Hills only twice each year.

Hoyt knew that in his travels, Kofi had experienced just about every job known to man, including working a stint as a leasing agent for a prominent resort company. Of course, he tried to keep his real job—a novelist who wrote shifter romances—a secret, but they all knew of his literary accomplishments. Hoyt had read them all many times. Kofi was the smartest shifter Hoyt had ever met, and there was nobody whose opinion Hoyt trusted more.

"Hello?" The voice on the other end of the line was low and silky.

Hoyt closed his eyes, picturing Kofi reclining in a lounger on a beach somewhere exotic, watching the sunset. In his imagination, Kofi wore loose shorts with a tropical pattern. His bare chest glistened in the setting sun, and those full lips closed over the long neck of a bottle of summer lager.

Hoyt's imagination was running away to a wonderful and forbidden place. He forced it to stop. "Kofi, this is Hoyt."

"I know." A smooth chuckle encouraged him to continue. "How are you?"

"I'm, um, I'm okay, I guess." Yep, now was an excellent time for Hoyt to turn into a stammering idiot. "How are you?"

"I'm well."

The other end went silent, reminding Hoyt that he was the one who'd called. "Look, I'm sorry to bother you, but I, um, I didn't know who else to call."

The wind and bird calls in the background went away. "What's wrong?"

Hoyt realized his hemming and hawing had triggered Kofi's worry buttons, and he scrambled to fix the situation. "Nothing's wrong. I was looking at real estate today because I'm thinking I want to open a coffee shop. You know, the kind that maybe serves parfaits or breakfast wraps or whatever I feel like making? I was thinking I'd keep it loose, like when customers come in, it'll be a surprise what's on the menu."

"Hoyt, take a breath." The worry in Kofi's tone was gone, replaced with a bit of humor.

Hoyt blushed, heat rising to suffuse his cheeks. He rambled. Words were his curse. When he was nervous or excited, they poured out of him at a million miles an hour. It had annoyed the hell out of Dak, and whenever Kofi had visited, Hoyt had struggled to slap a gag on his inner monologue that was often an outer one as well.

"Sorry. I shouldn't have called. I'm bothering you."

"You're not bothering me. I just don't want you passing out when there's no one around to catch you."

The heat in his cheeks flamed hotter. He'd love to protest that he wasn't that bad, but he regularly talked so much he made himself dizzy. "I'm lying back on a bed, so if that should happen, I'll be fine."

A groan came from the other end.

"Are you okay? Did I interrupt something? I can call back later, or never, if this is just too weird." The rules for contacting the brother of one's ex-husband were murky, at best. And if one had spent the past decade lusting after that man, then there were additional complications.

"You're fine. I'm hanging out alone tonight, and I had absolutely no plans. You're not interrupting anything."

"Oh." Hoyt had expected to have to cram his request into the space between breaths and then work a lot of begging in alongside it. "I don't know which one to lease."

"Which what?"

"Space. I spent the day looking at spaces to lease for my coffee shop, Grind-N-Growl."

"Grind-N-Growl?"

"Yes, you know, for coffee and bears?"

Kofi made a thoughtful noise. "Hoyt, don't take this the wrong way, but that names kind of sounds like a bar or dance club—a place people might go to hook up."

Two minutes ago, the name had a clever ring inside Hoyt's head. Now it wasn't so great. He wanted people to find their perfect mate, not hook up for a quick one-night stand. "Like, I'll hook them up with coffee?"

"Coffee is not the first thing that comes to mind." Kofi cleared his throat. "Where are you looking at leasing space?"

This was the part Hoyt didn't want to share, but he did it anyway, ripping off the figurative bandage. "Bear's Cove."

The line was too quiet.

"Hello? Kofi?" He looked at the screen to check the status of the connection. "Did the call drop?"

"I'm here." A growlish sigh came through. "Look, Hoyt, do you think that's a good idea? I mean, Dak's remarried, and he has a cub. I'm not sure what you hope to accomplish in Bear's Cove."

"Dak has nothing to do with it."

"No? Come on—anyone will see through that denial. What about Matunus Bay? It's a great town, and it's bigger than Bear's Cove, so there's more of a customer base."

Hoyt had lived in Matunus Bay for two months, and the place had never felt like home. The moment he'd come to Bear's Cove, he knew he'd arrived at his forever destination. "I don't expect you to understand, but I love it here. Dak has nothing to do with it. I swear." He'd talked to Chase about his idea. Dak's new husband seemed okay with it. He hadn't jumped for joy or offered to throw a housewarming party, but he hadn't been upset.

"Did you ask Dak?"

No, he hadn't asked Dak. His ex-husband would tell him to stay far away because he wouldn't want to take the chance his omega would be upset by it. That's why he'd talked to Chase. "Kofi, I called because I wanted your opinion on which lease I should take."

"Are you sure about that?"

Hoyt rarely lost his temper. He had a lot of patience, mostly because it took him time to stop talking and process what he'd heard. But Kofi was beating a dead horse. "You know what? You're right. I called to see if you could put in a good word for me. I've realized the error of my ways, and I want to get back into a loveless marriage with a guy who is totally unsuited to handle my energetic personality. I miss being miserable and making my husband equally miserable."

"Dak is a good person."

He'd struck a nerve. Kofi was a big brother, through-and-through. Nobody was allowed to criticize any of his family members. Hoyt blew out a stream of air. "I never said he wasn't. Not once. Not even when I asked him for a divorce. I told him he was a good person, and we both deserved better life partners."

"He's pretty awesome."

"Fucking hell, Kofi. Are you trying to convince me to give him another whirl? Because there's no way in hell that's happening. Maybe this arranged marriage business works for some bears, but it didn't work out for us—and I noticed that you, Ashwin, and Cruz avoided arranged marriages after that. I don't know what our fathers were drinking when they decided we were compatible, but we're not. So are you going to help me out by looking over the lease agreements, or are you just fucking with my mind?" At the end of all that, he remembered to breathe.

"Fucking with your mind?" Kofi chuckled. "I'll look over the leases after you get permission from Dak to open a business in Bear's Cove."

How dare that man laugh at him? The image of Kofi half-dressed vanished from Hoyt's brain in a puff of angry smoke. He sat forward and crossed his legs. "Fuck you, Kofi. He's not my alpha. I don't answer to him or to anyone else. Next time, just tell me you won't help out up front, okay? That'll save us both a lot of grief."

Hoyt ended the call and threw his phone down on the bed. Then he got up and paced the length of the room. Though he hadn't known what to expect from Kofi, the idea he'd accuse him of trying to get back with Dak hadn't occurred to him. He'd thought perhaps seeing Dak around town would be awkward, but it was a large enough place that they wouldn't necessarily need to run into one another, and when they did, they could be polite.

Their marriage had been a mistake. And to make matters worse, he'd spent the whole time lusting after Kofi. The brothers looked enough alike that it had been too easy to close his eyes and pretend he was with the brother who made his pulse race.

Hoyt booted up his laptop and spent the rest of the evening reading leases. It was better than talking to Kofi, but slightly less fun than dancing on a mound of fire ants.

Chapter 2—Kofi

The crack of dawn had nothing on Kofi. He'd slept poorly after that phone call from Hoyt. Seeing that name on his phone after all this time had affected him way too much. The idea of talking to his brother's ex-husband shouldn't bring a smile to his face.

And yet, it did. It always had, and that's why Kofi had moved away from Forrest Hills. The first time he'd seen the lanky redhead standing outside the café, his bear had noticed. Then the first time Hoyt had looked at him, those blue eyes had shot a cupid's bow straight into Kofi's heart. He'd wanted the omega for himself, but Hoyt had been engaged to his youngest brother. Kofi would rather die than hurt Dak.

He made coffee and tried to get some work done, but the words just wouldn't come. Unbeknownst to his family, he made a living writing romance novels, a profession he practiced in a series of exotic locations. He covered it up by working a series of odd and unusual jobs, most of which appeared in his books.

Though he gave it his best effort, today was a bust. Three mugs later, the sun had risen over the bay. He had a clear view from his small apartment overlooking Matunus Bay, and he'd imagined more than once what the rising or setting sun would look like glinting from Hoyt's ginger locks.

"There's nothing to do but go see him. Make it right."

Nobody was around to hear or answer him. He drained his mug and took a shower. If Hoyt slammed the door in his face, he was going to get a glimpse of Kofi at his best before he did it.

The drive to Bear's Cove took about forty minutes. The road connecting the two towns wound along the coast and sometimes disappeared into the trees. Their protected lands were beautiful and mostly untamed, and his inner bear appreciated it. Nowhere else in the world was like these lands. This was home, and Kofi was tired of traveling. He wanted to come home.

As he knocked on the door to Dak's house, he reflected that he should have called beforehand. Kofi wasn't the kind of man who showed up unannounced, though Dak wasn't the kind of man who would be upset by it. He didn't know Chase that well yet, but they had a baby, and Chase's great-grandmother lived with them. One of them might object, but it was too late now.

Simone answered the door. She'd raised Chase from the time his parents were killed when he was six years old. Though she was tiny and quite elderly, she was a force unto herself. She looked him up and down, her discerning gaze making Kofi shift uncomfortably. Perhaps he should have taken more time choosing his clothes? Was that a coffee stain on his pant leg?

A smile lit her face. "You're Kofi, right? It's been a few months since I've seen you, but I remember you were the one who looked the most like Dak."

Kofi returned her smile. "Nice to see you again, Simone. I dropped by to see Dak. I hope that's okay."

She chuckled. "Of course you're welcome. Dak will be happy to see you. He's in the living room with the baby."

She held the door open, and then she took his arm as she led him through a room he thought was the living room, through the kitchen, down a hall, and into another living room. The house was huge, and Kofi had forgotten Dak had purchased his new house with a growing family and an elderly grandparent in mind. Simone had her own suite, which gave her privacy and also kept her nearby in case she needed assistance.

"Ezra spent the night with me, and we got to playing this morning, so Dak joined us." Simone patted Kofi's hand. "Dak, look who came to see you."

Dak stood, lifting Ezra in his arms, and a huge grin lit his features. "Kofi, it's great to see you. What brings you by so bright and early?"

"I should have called." But he'd spent the forty minutes of the drive thinking about Hoyt and how he could've handled their conversation differently.

"It's fine. I have the morning off."

The pair embraced, and Ezra gripped Kofi's shirt. When he released his younger brother, Ezra clung to Kofi, and he came away with the child. He hugged his nephew closer and kissed the top of his blond head. "He's getting so big."

"He's sitting up by himself, though he falls over a lot still." A small chuckle fell from Dak. He was probably picturing Ezra toppling as he tried to reach for a toy, or something else baby-related. "Chase is in the shower. He'll be down soon."

Simone stroked the top of Ezra's head. "Why don't you three go have coffee or something? This old lady needs a nap."

Dak's expression sobered. "Are you feeling okay?"

11

"Just tired. This little one isn't much for sleeping. He kept waking me up by laughing in his crib. He just lays there and giggles. It's the cutest thing."

Dak pressed a kiss to Simone's cheek. "Call if you need anything."

"I will." She shooed them from her suite.

Carrying his nephew, Kofi followed his brother down the hall and into the kitchen. "Do you think it's wise to let Ezra stay with her if he's going to interfere with her sleep?"

"I know better than to tell Simone she can't have a sleepover with Ezra." Dak poured water into the coffee maker. "She loves Ezra, and he adores her."

Kofi peered toward the hall and lowered his voice. "But she's so old. Can she physically handle caring for a baby?"

"She does fine. Ezra is an easy baby, and Simone has a device that alerts us if she needs help."

As if to reinforce claims of his affable nature, Ezra flapped his arms and let out a screaming laugh. Once he had Kofi's attention, his smile only grew. "Hi, Ezra. How about we be quiet so your great-great-grandmother can take a nap?"

More laughter rolled from Ezra, and it was contagious. Kofi found himself smiling and chuckling along with the infant.

"She can sleep through just about anything when she's not babysitting, so he's okay." Dak set a mug of coffee in front of Kofi but still out of reach of the baby. "What's up?"

Now that he was here, Kofi didn't want to talk about what had brought him so far on a whim. "I need to have a reason to visit my brother and my only nephew?"

"You don't." Dak sipped. "Most people who drive forty minutes to get somewhere have an ulterior motive. Don't get me wrong—I love that you're here, but I know you're not here just to see me."

That made him sound like a shitty brother. He made a face at Ezra, eliciting more laughter and arm flapping. "Maybe I came for this little cup of joy."

Dak considered this. "Did you?"

He sighed. "No, but this is a pleasant bonus."

"Are you hungry? Did you have breakfast?"

"I ate early, so I'll be hungry again soon." Kofi grinned. He loved to eat.

Chase sailed into the room. He ruffled Kofi's hair, dropped a kiss on Ezra's cheek, and then he kissed Dak. It was open-mouthed and passionate, leaving Kofi feeling a little like a voyeur.

12

He made more faces at Ezra while his brother engaged in an extended display of affection with his omega. He'd certainly never seen Dak do that with Hoyt. Come to think of it, he couldn't remember Dak and Hoyt kissing with any kind of spontaneity. Their partings had been marked by perfunctory pecks on the cheek, though after a time, those had disappeared as well.

"Good morning, Kofi. It's great to see you. Did I hear you say you wanted some breakfast?"

He lifted a shoulder and smiled at his brother-in-law. "I wouldn't say no to whatever you're thinking of making."

Chase ran a hand through his short blond locks, and joy danced in his light brown eyes. "Pancakes and sausage. I love sausage."

Fire flashed in Dak's eyes. "Later, cub. Just you wait."

"Yes, Daddy." Though he'd started it, a light blush stained Chase's cheeks. He went to the cabinet and took out a mixing bowl and a pan.

They chatted, talking about Kofi's travels, Dak and Chase's life events, and Ezra's growth and development. Time flew, and before Kofi knew it, the meal was over.

"That hit the spot. Thanks, Chase."

Chase collected a yawning Ezra. "Time for your nap, little man. We'll leave Dad and Uncle Kofi to do the dishes."

When he was gone, Kofi gathered dishes from the table. "You seem happy."

With a more vibrant expression than Kofi had ever seen on his brother, Dak took glasses to the counter. "I am happier than I ever imagined possible." He threw a hand towel over his shoulder and turned on the faucet. "But you, my brother, aren't. What's wrong?"

As Kofi wrapped the extra pancakes for storage, he struggled to find the words. "Nothing really."

Dak didn't say anything. Water ran, a soothing sound that forced Kofi to sigh.

"Hoyt called me last night."

"Yeah?" Dak seemed puzzled. "What did he want?"

"He wanted me to read over some leasing contracts."

"Makes sense. If I were going to lease a property, I'd want your advice." Dak loaded the last plate into the dishwasher. "Are you upset because he called you?"

"No."

"Good. He doesn't really have anyone else to ask. His fathers sucked at deal-making, and Hoyt's brother wouldn't have a clue about real estate or contracts. He's only eighteen." Dak started on the flatware. "I don't think any of his friends would know anything, either."

Kofi set the pancake pan on the counter next to the sink. "You're really okay with him calling me?"

Dak shrugged. "Just because it didn't work out between him and me doesn't mean he isn't a good person. In fact, if he hadn't divorced me, we'd both still be living in misery." He spread his hands wide. "I partially have him to thank for all of this. I never would have come to Bear's Cove to pursue my dream of being a deputy, and I never would have met Chase or had Ezra. It's okay for you to be friends with him."

This was a topic that Kofi had assiduously avoided discussing with Dak. "Are you friends with him?"

"Friends—that's a bit of a stretch. We're friendly and cordial, but it's not like I see him very often." Dak chuckled. "Of course, you never could stand Hoyt for very long, so maybe I should have said you could continue to be polite to him."

Kofi's head swiveled with surprise. "What makes you think I couldn't stand Hoyt? I liked him just fine." Too fine—he'd lusted after and fantasized about him.

Dak's eyebrows lifted. "Whenever his mouth got going, you didn't last more than five minutes in a room with him. I knew not to leave you two alone because I was afraid I'd come back to find him tied to a chair with duct tape over his mouth."

The idea of Hoyt tied up had some merit, but not in the way Dak thought. Kofi huffed. "I would never have done that."

"Look, I'm just saying he hasn't changed. He's still the same impulsive, effervescent, energetic guy he's always been. He can fill a room by himself, and that's always driven you away." The water shut off, and Dak faced him. "I'm not ignorant of the reasons you stayed away while I was with him. Hoyt's incessant chatter drove you nuts, and the more annoyed you got, the more nervous he got, and so he talked more. It was a vicious cycle."

Sometimes Hoyt talked too much, but that had never annoyed Kofi. The longer he was with Hoyt, the more insistent his bear became. He'd removed himself from temptation so he wouldn't do something stupid and heartless like betray his brother. "It wasn't that bad. His constant chatter didn't seem to annoy you."

"I tuned him out." Dak's lips twisted wryly. "It was a bad relationship from the start."

Kofi contemplated a fifth mug of coffee, but he was already jittery. "Not like what you have with Chase."

"It's nothing like what I have with Chase. I can listen to him talk about fixing lawn mowers for hours. It's not the topic I care about; it's Chase's enthusiasm and interest that keeps my attention." Dak shook his head. "Listen, I'm not going to tell you what to do, but if Hoyt swallowed his pride enough to ask you for help, then he really needs it."

The idea of the omega floundering all alone with no alpha to save him tugged at Kofi's heartstrings. But there was still one more issue. "He wants to open a coffee shop in Bear's Cove. I suggested he look in another town, and he hung up on me."

Dak bit his lip in a failed attempt to squelch the laughter. At least it came out quietly. "Like I said, he's impulsive. He's also moody and bratty. Your call if you want to deal with that."

"Did you ever take him in hand?" Not having been around, Kofi had no idea what had transpired between Dak and Hoyt.

"Nope." Dak pressed his lips together and shook his head. "I did my thing, and I let him do his thing."

The main issue still had not been addressed. "But are you okay with him following you to Bear's Cove?"

Dak ran his hand through his dark hair that was so like Kofi's. "I'm fine with Hoyt doing his thing wherever he wants. He's good-hearted and mostly harmless. The only thing I worry about is Chase."

The object of Dak's concern padded into the room on silent feet. He glanced around, taking in the clean kitchen, and then he slipped his arm around Dak's waist. "Thanks for cleaning up, and don't worry about me. Hoyt already called me about opening a coffee shop in Bear's Cove. He said he loves it here, but he didn't want to move here if it would be too weird."

Surprise widened Dak's eyes and Kofi echoed his brother's shock. Why hadn't Hoyt informed him of this last night? It would have allayed his unease and kept him from losing a night's sleep.

"When did he call you?" Kofi asked.

"A few weeks ago. He's a talker, that one." Chase grinned. "I like him, but I think he's best in small doses. Ezra and I met him for lunch a couple days ago when he got to town."

Dak frowned. "Why haven't you told me any of this?"

Chase pressed his front to Dak's side, and his lips turned up in a coy smile. "Because I'm a bad, bad cub, and I need a spanking."

"Seriously." Though Dak crossed his arms, Kofi could tell he was moments from pulling his omega closer. "Why?"

This time Chase lifted a shoulder. "I was going to tell you about the call, but it slipped my mind. Then with the lunch date, I came home to find you naked with a tray of chocolate-covered strawberries. It made me forget to talk to you about your ex."

Dak contemplated that silently.

Chase smiled at Kofi. "He's trying to justify still giving me a spanking." He put his hand to one side of his mouth and whispered. "Like he needs a reason."

Kofi motioned to the door. "I'm going to get out of here and let you two enjoy the rest of Ezra's nap. I'll call later."

"He's at the Black Bear Inn." Chase lifted onto his tiptoes and nuzzled into Dak's neck as he threw out that information.

"Thanks. I'll lock the front door on my way out." Kofi loved that his brother had found his perfect mate.

He programmed the Black Bear Inn into his navigation and set a course for the hotel where Hoyt was staying.

Chapter 3—Hoyt

Though the Black Bear Inn was nestled in the hills, it had a clear view of the cove. Hoyt had stayed up late reading contracts. Most of the text made sense to him, but there were a few parts he didn't understand. Sure, he'd looked up the meaning, but he didn't understand enough about real estate law to comprehend the intent of certain clauses.

It looked like he was going to have to ask Ulysses what some things meant. That was no big deal. After all, he was paying Ulysses to look out for his best interest. He'd just feel better with advice from someone he already trusted.

Hoyt slept late, and after a leisurely lunch, he went for a swim in the cold waters of the cove. As he dove beneath the waves, he thought about the various properties, running through a pro/con list in his head. If he leased the property down the street that backed up to the rocky shoreline, he could be right on the beach. That meant he could go for a swim whenever he got a break. It also meant people who were cold from swimming or surfing could warm up with a beverage from his establishment. And it would be perfect for the matchmaking parties he wanted to have. Potential couples could go for a moonlit stroll on the beach while they got to know each other.

The second of the properties was on Main Street. Centrally located, it boasted access to people hanging around downtown, and it wasn't far from the shore. It was also ideal for hit matchmaking events because it was in the heart of town. But there were three other coffee shops in that stretch already. Hoyt didn't have the cash to hire a big firm to come in and see if the market was already saturated. He needed to make sure the location he chose would be good for business. He needed foot traffic, and he also needed a way for people to drop by to pick up a quick cup of coffee. The third location, on the edge of town, would target people driving through the area and anyone who lived farther from the cove. Those were the kinds of people who didn't necessarily like to hang out downtown all the time. It would take some serious advertising to pull shifters in for his matchmaking parties, but once he got it going, it wouldn't be too difficult to maintain.

After a half hour, he headed back to the inn. Having the complexion that accompanied being a ginger, he knew better than to tempt fate. Even with sunscreen, he was prone to burning. Due to the hilly and rocky terrain, The Black Bear Inn was a collection of small buildings that had been turned into a resort. The building where Hoyt had his room also housed three other rooms, all of which could be accessed from the outside.

He dried most of the water from his body before he got back, and he stopped short at the door to his room.

A man lounged against his door, his wide shoulders spanning most of the distance. His body narrowed where he'd tucked his shirt into jeans, showcasing the powerful muscles of his hips and thighs.

Hoyt's gaze roved down and back up, taking in the full lips and how the wind lifted strands of black hair, messing them up in a way that only increased his sexiness. Then he took off his sunglasses, and Hoyt found himself nailed to the spot by those brilliant blue eyes. The sky reflected in them, casting them an even darker hue.

He sucked in a breath and forced his body not to respond. This was just like every fucking holiday and family-oriented get-together for six of the past seven years. He'd forgotten the physical way his body reacted to Kofi, and it irritated him. "What do you want?" A bit of that annoyance came out in his voice, but he didn't care. Kofi had it coming.

He moved away from the door, which put him closer to Hoyt. "Why didn't you tell me that you'd talked to Chase?"

Hoyt rolled his eyes and moved past Kofi. He stuck the key in the lock, but it wouldn't turn. So now his attempt to make a dramatic getaway was ruined. He jiggled the handle and tried again, but it didn't work.

Kofi's hand closed around Hoyt's as he took over. His jiggling worked better, and the lock disengaged. He pushed the door open, stepped back, and handed the key to Hoyt.

When Hoyt tried to grab it back, Kofi held tight to the part of the key ring with a dangling thingy printed with The Black Bear Inn's logo. A warning flashed in his eyes, the kind that might have him on his knees if the circumstances were different. "Hoyt, don't be pissy. I had a legitimate concern."

Hoyt parked his free hand on his hip. "Let go of my fucking keys. I didn't ask you to come here, and I don't owe you an explanation. You're not my alpha."

"You asked me for a favor."

At the reminder, heat traveled up Hoyt's neck. Fucking fair skin got blotchy whenever he got mad. "You said no, and I moved on."

"I didn't say no. I told you to clear it with Dak first. It wasn't an unreasonable condition."

18

Rather than continue this pointless fight, Hoyt rolled his eyes and went into his room. He scooped up a pair of clean shorts and went into the bathroom. Soon he had the shower going, and the warm spray washed the salt off his skin. He heard the door to his room close, and the tension went out of his body. Kofi was gone, taking with him most of Hoyt's stress, but he'd left behind an aching sense of loss. Perhaps calling Kofi for help had been a mistake. Seeing him again definitely was.

Freshly cleaned, Hoyt got out of the shower. He muttered to himself while he dried off, complaints about Kofi mixing with the items on his pro/con list for each possible location.

He tugged his shorts on and emerged from the bathroom, drying his hair with the towel as he thought about what shirt he wanted to wear. Rounding the corner separating the bathroom and kitchenette from the part of the room meant for sleep, Hoyt stopped short at the sight of Kofi lounging on the bed.

Kofi sat up as Hoyt froze, steely determination in the set of his shoulders. "I'm not leaving without an answer."

"I didn't invite you in." Catty, sure, but Hoyt wasn't the kind of man who was up for verbal sparring. Not only did Kofi knock him off kilter with his mere presence, but Hoyt hadn't prepared for this conversation. When Kofi used to visit during the holidays, Hoyt had ample time to rehearse conversations on a variety of topics.

Kofi's gaze moved up and down Hoyt's body, reminding him that he was *sans* shirt. And, with the power of a soft caress, that gaze stirred Hoyt's slumbering bear.

To combat that urge, Hoyt snagged the nearest shirt, one he'd already worn and hadn't yet laundered, and he jammed his arms into it. "I don't know why you drove all the way out here to confront me. I mean, it's a little overboard, don't you think? Where were you, anyway? I know you don't live here or visit here very often. Chase said he'd only met you a couple of times, which made sense because I only ever saw you at holidays or during that cookout your fathers used to have every summer where they'd roast a whole elk or moose or something. You guys were all big eaters, so there was never much in the way of leftovers. Which was good, I guess. Less to put away, and Abe and I always got stuck with that part of cleanup."

Kofi got to his feet, and he touched the tip of his finger to Hoyt's lips, halting the flow of words. "I came here to read the contracts you asked me to read."

When Kofi's finger dropped away, Hoyt spoke. "Oh. You could have done that from wherever you were. I could have emailed them."

Thoughts always came out Hoyt's mouth rather than rattle around in his head. This was a problem Dak had discussed with him *ad nauseum* while they'd been married. "You didn't have to drop everything and drive or fly all the way here. I mean, there's no reason, not unless—"

Once again, Kofi's fingertip rested against Hoyt's lips, and without the chatter to distract him, he was acutely aware of the strength simmering behind the soft warning. "I was in Matunus Bay, so I wasn't all that far away. I know you're upset because I wanted you to get Dak's approval first, but please try to understand my position."

Hoyt rolled his eyes and moved out of Kofi's reach. "I don't fucking care about your position. This is my life. I divorced your brother because I didn't want him to have a say in my life, and I sure as hell am not giving you a say in anything I do." He parked his hands on his hips and channeled the best of his inner diva. "Newsflash, Kofi—the world doesn't revolve around the Freeman brothers. I'm so sick of you and your fathers trying to tell me what I can and can't do with my life. It's none of your fucking business. You don't want to help me out, then don't help, but you don't get to tell me what I can and can't do."

Something dark and dangerous flashed in Kofi's eyes.

This was an expression Hoyt had never seen before, and it alarmed him because he didn't know exactly what it meant. He shrank back a step and held up a hand. "I didn't ask you to come in here, either. You can't stop me from opening my coffee shop."

"You know what your problem is?" Though the warning didn't fade from Kofi's damning blue eyes, his tone was conversational. "You don't listen when other people speak. You talk right over them."

Yeah, this had been a frequent discussion topic when he'd been married to Dak. Hoyt rolled his eyes and flounced away.

He didn't get far. Kofi's hand wrapped around his upper arm, an iron band that jerked him back around and forced him to face the angry alpha who didn't belong to him.

"Mostly," Kofi continued, his tone even softer, "you suffer from never having been spanked."

Hoyt sucked in a breath. Nobody had ever laid a violent hand on him, not his parents, and not his ex-alpha. "You wouldn't."

"I would." He closed the distance, his volume dropping to almost subsonic levels and his breath fanning over Hoyt's cheek. "I'd even enjoy it."

Hoyt believed Kofi would carry out his threat. Part of him was curious about the whole concept, part of him was afraid, and part of him hoped Kofi liked his ass. He'd never been so flummoxed before. He drew in a breath and called the alpha's bluff. "I'll scream."

One corner of Kofi's mouth curved in a sinful smile. "I'll hang out the Do Not Disturb sign." He released his hold in a gentle slide that seemed almost like a caress. "Take your shorts off."

Hoyt watched Kofi go into the hall. He heard the door open and close, and the snick of the lock sealed his fate. Last night he'd used all his courage to call Kofi for advice, and today he was minutes from getting his backside blistered by a man he'd only fantasized about.

Kofi returned, padding back on bare feet. He adjusted the pillows on the bed Hoyt had made that morning. Then he climbed on, centering himself with a pillow at his back and one on his legs. He gestured for Hoyt to lay across his lap.

"I don't have to do this." Though his throat was dry and his tongue felt thick, words tumbled out. His brain was constantly working, and the words falling from his lips were the byproduct of an overactive brain. They rarely deserted him.

"No, you don't," Kofi said. His low tone washed over Hoyt's senses, lulling the worst of his panic. "You can ask me to leave, and I will."

He'd dreamed so long of this—well, maybe not exactly this, but mostly this. Almost in a trance, he found himself moving toward Kofi. He knelt on the bed, and then he settled on the pillow over the alpha's lap.

He felt Kofi's hands at his hips.

"Lift up."

He did, and his shorts eased down, revealing his pale ass. It was too pale. The glare would blind Kofi. Suddenly Hoyt was self-conscious. He reached down to pull up his shorts, but Kofi pushed his hands away.

"Keep them above your head, or I will bind them."

Under other circumstances, being tied up with Kofi in charge could be fun, but Hoyt didn't get the sense this was one of those times. He raised his arms.

"Spread your legs, and get your knees under you a bit." Kofi helped him into the position he wanted.

Then he felt Kofi's hand on his ass, rubbing circles over the pristine flesh.

All of a sudden, butterflies rampaged in his stomach. "Are you sure you want to do this? I mean, we could talk about it."

"No talking, Hoyt. You can cry out if you need to, but I must insist you don't talk otherwise." Kofi's caresses increased in pressure, and Hoyt's dick jerked in response.

He buried his face in the bedspread and groaned.

"Good boy. Let's start with ten."

The first swat landed on Hoyt's right cheek, and the sting took a moment to register. The second followed on the left. Sensations bloomed, too many for Hoyt to process. Each time Kofi's hand connected with his flesh, a whimper sounded in Hoyt's throat. By the time the fifth one landed, all thoughts had fled. For the first time in his life, his brain was blessedly bereft of words and stress.

It ended before he could come to terms with any of it, but since his brain had shut off, he didn't move.

Kofi's hand moved over his skin, the soft caress so at odds with the violence of what he'd just done. "So fair. I can see my handprints perfectly. I almost hate to cover it up." With a pleased sigh, Kofi scooted Hoyt's shorts back in place. He lifted Hoyt, turning him over and cradling him in his lap. "How do you feel?"

Hoyt peered up at Kofi and blinked. He knew he had a wide, dumb expression on his face, but he didn't know how to shield his emotions from the man who'd just spanked him.

Kofi caressed Hoyt's cheek, a feathery stroke that made Hoyt's breath catch. Maybe he would have been fine if Kofi hadn't been so fucking gentle and tender. The brutality of the spanking was at odds with the expression on his face and the way he touched Hoyt.

Without thinking—because his brain was still on hiatus—Hoyt flung his head toward Kofi, mashing his lips to the alpha's.

For a hot second, Kofi froze. Then his mouth moved. He captured Hoyt's lips, taking over the kiss. Hoyt clutched at Kofi's shoulder as sharp points of desire seared from his backside and through his body. He moaned and straddled Kofi's legs.

Kofi ripped the pillow on his lap away. One hand threaded into Hoyt's hair, holding him still for the onslaught of the kiss that didn't sate either of them, and the other cruised down Hoyt's back. It settled on his tender ass, gripping hard and pressing Hoyt closer.

Hoyt's bear rose to the fore, and the deep whimper that escaped was how he offered himself to this virile alpha. Kofi's bear answered with a growl. His caresses roughened as his hands slid under Hoyt's shirt. It lifted on an impatient gesture, and Hoyt helped slide it over his head.

Before the fabric cleared his field of vision, Kofi's teeth sank into his nipple. Hoyt cried out, his hands gripping Kofi's massive shoulders to ease the pain.

"Breathe through it." Kofi's voice was as rough as the hands moving over his body grabbing handfuls of flesh wherever it could. He'd issued the directive without taking his teeth from Hoyt's flesh.

Hoyt breathed, and as the pain lessened, pleasure flooded his body, and he moaned.

Kofi's tongue lathed away the sting. "Good boy. Let's do the other one."

"Yes, Daddy." He spoke without thinking, using the term he'd swallowed down for so long.

Kofi glanced up, but he didn't otherwise react to the moniker.

Though he knew what to expect, Hoyt still gasped when Kofi bit the other nipple. Rather than try to push away from the larger man, he sank his fingers into Kofi's thick locks. For years, he'd imagined the silky slide through his fingers, and now he luxuriated in the dual sensations.

The pressure of the bite eased, and Kofi lifted Hoyt, laying him on his back. Hoyt peeled away Kofi's shirt as the alpha repositioned himself between Hoyt's legs. Faced with the bare expanse of chest, Hoyt's breath stopped. Kofi was even more magnificent than he remembered.

"You are so fucking sexy." He ran his hands over Kofi's shoulders and arms before traveling down his chest.

On his hands and knees, Kofi leaned down and nipped at Hoyt's lips. "If you don't stop me, Hoyt, I'm going to fuck you. I want to see if an orgasm turns your face and chest as red as that spanking turned your luscious ass."

Just hearing that sentiment sent heat traveling to Hoyt's neck and face. "Red is sort of my color."

Amusement stretched Kofi's mouth a second before it met Hoyt's for a fiery kiss. They powered on, full steam ahead—tearing at remaining clothes until they were both naked. Kofi kissed his way down Hoyt's neck, licking and sucking until he was faced with evidence of Hoyt's arousal. His dick sprang from a nest of amber curls, the purpled head lending a bit of rainbow to the color mix.

Kofi wrapped a hand around Hoyt's balls as he licked the underside of Hoyt's cock. Though he didn't mean to, Hoyt compared Kofi to Dak—particularly Dak's love of cock-and-ball torture. It looked like the brothers had some things in common. Knowing what came next, Hoyt relaxed his upper body back and let his legs fall open.

The pressure in his balls changed as Kofi pulled on the sac. Waves of pleasure washed through Hoyt as the tugging sensation increased. He moaned loudly, and he whimpered as the tension eased.

"Do you like that?" Kofi's tongue swirled around the head of Hoyt's cock.

"Yes, Daddy." He gasped because Kofi had begun to pull at his sac again. "A lot."

23

With that affirmation, Kofi played around. He tugged handfuls as his head bobbed on Hoyt's dick. It felt so fucking good, all sorts of strange pleasure that stole his ability to think and reason. And it had been so long since Hoyt had allowed a man in his bed. His balls drew up, which sent shards of delicious pleasure cresting through him because Kofi was pulling in the opposite direction, and an orgasm robbed him of even the ability to moan.

Kofi loomed over him, his handsome visage filling Hoyt's field of vision. Riding the waves of his climax, he could do nothing but stare at the man who'd spanked his ass and sucked his cock.

He reached up to wipe away a bit of spittle or semen from Kofi's lip, and the alpha's tongue shot out to lick Hoyt's finger.

Hoyt smiled. "Thank you for that. It was incredible. I hope you're not finished with me."

A sly grin was his response.

"I have lube in my suitcase. I'll go grab it."

Kofi stilled him by laying his heavier body on top. "Have you ever climaxed like that before?"

Shades of shock manifested as coldness in his chest. "Maybe let's not talk about my sexual history, okay?"

Understanding dawned like a blinding day on Kofi's face. His gaze sidled away as if he'd just realized he was in the midst of fucking his brother's ex. "Oh, yeah. I guess that's weird."

"A little bit." Hoyt ran his fingers through Kofi's hair once again. "It'd probably be really weird if I told you I'd fantasized about this for years."

Kofi's head cocked to the side as he considered it. "About as weird as it's been for me to lust after my brother's husband all those years."

"Really?" Hoyt hadn't expected the yearning to have been two-sided.

"Yeah. That's mostly why I stayed away."

The sad confession hit Hoyt like a punch to the gut. "I'm sorry if I came between you and your family."

Kofi rested his forehead against Hoyt's. "You didn't do anything wrong. And if what we're doing right now is wrong, I don't want to be right."

With his best and most flamboyant grin, Hoyt said, "Me, neither. Let me go grab that lube. I want to feel you inside me."

With a permissive nod, Kofi rolled to the side. Hoyt sprang from the bed and rummaged through his suitcase for lube. If he remembered correctly, it was in with the toiletries. He hadn't expected to have sex on this trip, but it was part of his travel kit, so it traveled with him. Rifling through clothes didn't turn up the kit, and neither did opening every single zippered pouch on his suitcase or his other pieces of luggage. Had he taken it into the bathroom? Maybe. He hurried to find out.

Jackpot.

When he emerged triumphantly a few minutes later, he found Kofi lounging on the bed and staring at the ceiling. He was bored.

Hoyt realized he'd taken more than a few minutes to find the lube. "What? Are you mad? It's not like I was expecting to use it. If I want to masturbate, I have lotion."

A huge grin split Kofi's face, and he held out a hand. "You are so freaking adorable. Come here."

He climbed on the bed, walking closer on his knees, and he handed over the lube.

Kofi set it off to the side and crooked his finger, beckoning Hoyt closer. Hoyt bent down, and he was rewarded with a tender kiss. Though it was sweet and heartfelt, it didn't take long to spark the passion that had been simmering below the surface for too many years. Kofi dragged Hoyt to him until he toppled onto the alpha, and then he wrapped his arms around him as he masterfully controlled the kiss.

They kissed and caressed until Hoyt was hard again, and they were both trembling. Then Kofi rolled until he was on top, and he urged Hoyt's legs apart.

Out of his mind with need, Hoyt snagged the bottle of lube and squirted some onto his palm. He grasped Kofi's throbbing member in his hand, massaging lube onto the shaft until Kofi stayed his hand.

Reaching down, Kofi touched Hoyt's sphincter, oiling it up with lube from his own cock. His fingers pressed forward, breaching that tender opening and eliciting a gasp from Hoyt. When the tip of Kofi's cock nudged open that protective muscle, Hoyt exhaled to allow him entry.

Kofi's cock filled him.

"Oh, Daddy, that feels so good." He moaned at the fullness, and his eyes rolled back in his head. Nothing in his life had ever felt so unbelievably good. He fit like he'd been made to be there.

"Open your eyes." Kofi's order cut through the haze that enveloped Hoyt. "Look at me."

Forcing his eyelids to open, he focused on the man responsible for the spine-tingling pleasure rioting in his core.

"Say my name."

"Kofi." He whispered it reverently, a verbal caress.

"Again."

He said it again, forcing it out louder because he wanted nothing more than to please this alpha. His alpha. If he never again had the pleasure and the privilege of being in Kofi's arms, this memory was going to have to warm up a lot of lonely nights. Because no matter what happened, he never wanted to be with another man. This was it for Hoyt.

"Beg me to fuck you."

"Please," he breathed. "Daddy, please fuck me."

Kofi withdrew, and then he thrust deep. "Do you want more, Hoyt? Do you?"

"Yes, oh, yes."

"Say my name."

"Fuck me, Kofi. Fuck me hard and fast and soft and slow. I don't care how you do it as long as you're fucking me. Please, Kofi, please."

The words fueled Kofi. A fire lit behind his eyes, and the flame burned brighter the more Hoyt begged. So he set his tongue free and let words fall from his lips. He begged and pleaded. He whispered, gasped, and shouted Kofi's name, watching as it stoked his lover's passions.

When he was out of his mind and so close to orgasm, he felt Kofi's hand on his cock. "Come with me. Now."

His body responded to the alpha's order, and with a guttural cry, he came. His orgasm detonated, shattering the shell around his heart. When he came down, he found Kofi's arms wrapped around him, and their bodies curved together.

Chapter 4—Kofi

He dressed slowly, reluctant to leave the cocoon they'd created. Hoyt was everything he'd imagined, and so much more. His kisses drew Kofi in and made him never want to stop. The feel of his hands on Kofi's skin transported him to a haven containing only the two of them. Hoyt's passionate nature stroked the bear deep inside Kofi, settling him down for the first time since he'd set eyes upon the younger shifter.

They'd spent the day having sex and talking real estate. Kofi wasn't a real estate lawyer, but he had a lot of experience with leasing and contracts, and he possessed an intuitive intelligence that had served him well his whole life. He'd given his honest opinion, and now Hoyt sat cross-legged on the bed, printed contracts scattered around him.

Kofi sat on a chair and stared at Hoyt. He was a vision in a white robe. It brought out the blond highlights in his ginger hair and the crystal blue of his eyes. He had a strong jaw, the kind that invited nibbling, and his lips were the color of barely ripened strawberries. After a lot of kissing, their color deepened to ripe strawberries.

He wanted to push aside those papers and sample Hoyt's kiss, but he forced himself to loosen his shoelaces so he could put them on.

Hoyt glanced up, his gaze moving over Kofi. "Are you running out to get dinner?"

Unable to meet the questions in Hoyt's eyes, he shook his head. "I have a long drive back. I need to get going."

A teasing grin lit Hoyt's entire face. "Oh, Daddy. You can stay the night if you want."

That title. Conflicting emotions battled in Kofi. On one hand, he identified as a Daddy, and he loved hearing Hoyt use the title. On the other hand—had he used that title with Dak? After all, that's what Chase called Dak now. He shoved it all aside because he had more pressing matters to think about.

For example, he had to answer Hoyt's invitation. Should he lie and tell Hoyt he had to work in the morning? No—he owed him the truth. He slid his shoes on and focused on tying his shoelaces. "I'm—um—I'm supposed to meet Dak and Chase for dinner." He ran a hand through his hair and stood up. "I didn't mean—This wasn't supposed to—I thought I was coming over here to read contracts."

All traces of happiness vanished from Hoyt's face. The lines of his body stiffened, and his lips thinned. "Yeah, I get it. This was a one-day-stand—sex with the brother's ex. It was fun to let off some steam, and now it's time to go back to our regularly scheduled lives."

Kofi crossed his arms as if the pose could deflect the anger and hurt Hoyt tried to hide behind his offhand tone. He cleared his throat. "Hoyt, I didn't mean—"

Leaping from the bed, Hoyt landed on the floor in one graceful move of his lithe, limber body. Anger suffused his features and ruddied his skin. He pointed a sharp finger at Kofi, but he didn't make physical contact. "Fuck you, Kofi. The door is that way."

Giving in to his primal side, he grabbed Hoyt by the arms and drew him closer. "We had a nice time today. I didn't come here knowing any of this would happen. I made these plans before you kissed me. I don't regret what happened between us, but I also don't know what's next—and neither do you."

"I know what's next." Hoyt's natural effervescence had been extinguished. The sparkle was gone from his eyes, and his mouth set in a grim line. "You're leaving. I'd thank you for helping me, but I think I already took care of that."

He tried to appeal to Hoyt's common sense. "Don't say that."

Hoyt crossed his arms, his jaw set hard. "Goodbye, Kofi. Thank you for coming by. I enjoyed spending time with you, and I understand that you don't want to be late for your dinner plans."

The words were right, but the tone was wrong. Kofi wanted to stay, but he also knew it was pointless. They had no future together. And so he headed out the door.

That evening at dinner, the scene with Hoyt kept replaying in his head. He didn't know what else he could have said. Nothing was going to change the fact that Hoyt had been married to Kofi's brother, which meant he was permanently off-limits—the slip-up this afternoon notwithstanding.

It was a good thing Dak and Chase were so wrapped up in each other. They didn't notice Kofi was a poor dining companion, or if they did, they didn't make an issue of it.

On the way out, Dak loaded Chase into their truck. "Hey," he called to Kofi. "Wait up."

With the door to his sedan open, he waited for his brother who was parked three cars over. "Miss me already?"

Dak flashed a tired smile. "Of course. I wanted to ask about how today went, but I didn't want to bring it up with Chase there."

Kofi lifted his eyebrows. "Because you think he doesn't know you're talking about it now?"

"He's the one who told me to ask."

With a laugh, Kofi clapped Dak on the shoulder. "You have your hands full."

"No doubt, but how did it go?"

Kofi shrugged. There was no way he was telling Dak he'd spent the day fucking his ex-husband. "I read contracts. He decided on a property."

"No drama?"

Drama had been part of the action. Hoyt had been hot under the collar when he'd arrived, but he'd settled down nicely. The evening sun dipped behind the mountains, and a cool breeze blew in from the ocean. There were parts of the day he wanted to keep to himself. They were precious and meaningful, even if they'd been temporary. "He's not that bad, Dak. Actually, he's a pretty decent person."

"I know." Dak frowned. "I also know he has a diva temper, and the fact that you wanted him to run it by me before he moved to Bear's Cove would set him off. You're not the kind of person who has patience for that kind of drama."

Kofi was amazed Dak had put up with it, but given that Hoyt had experienced his first spanking earlier that day, Dak had evidently let him get away with throwing temper tantrums. "Maybe I'm better at handling him than you were."

"Ouch." Dak's wince had a dramatic flair. "That was harsh, brother of mine. But I've learned, and I'm not making the same mistakes with Chase."

Chase wasn't a diva, and so he wasn't high-maintenance. That was perfect for Dak, but Kofi preferred Hoyt's flair for the dramatic.

They embraced, and Kofi headed back to his apartment in Matunus Bay.

It took him a week to cave to the urge to call Hoyt. During that time, he'd missed the omega like crazy. He'd invaded Kofi's dreams, and he'd become the omega hero of the current work in progress. This was not a new phenomenon, but now Kofi had memory and experience

29

on which to base it. Descriptions of the taste of Hoyt's skin and the softness of his lips made it into the manuscript.

He'd texted Hoyt a few times, but the stubborn omega hadn't responded.

Hoyt didn't pick up when he called, so he left a message. "I'm wondering how it went with the lease? Did you get the one you chose?"

The next day, he checked his phone. Nothing from Hoyt, so he called again. "If you're looking to piss me off, this is a stellar way to do it. If you're trying for another spanking, keep it up. I'll find you, and I'll turn your ass bright red. That's a promise."

Neither the polite inquiry nor the threat produced a response. Was it stalking if he tracked Hoyt down in search of a reply?

It was probably something illegal. At best, it was a desperate move, and Kofi hated desperate heroes. He preferred leading men who were strong and self-assured. They knew how to take decisive action, and their omegas always welcomed their guidance.

Hoyt was headstrong, and Kofi had watched him reject Dak's alpha nature. What made him think one afternoon of sexcapades changed anything between them? He'd been the one who'd insisted it didn't—and couldn't.

Would Dak care if he dated Hoyt?

His brother had moved on. He was happily married, and they had a baby they both adored. There was no way Dak spent any time thinking about Hoyt.

Not like Kofi, who spent every waking moment with that slice of strawberry hotness on his mind.

Kofi threw a bag together. He packed lube, handcuffs, a dildo, and a blindfold. Just to be safe, he threw in a flogger and a paddle. He stared at the contents of the bag and perched his hands on his hips. "I'll show you how to answer your fucking phone."

Then he threw in a change of clothes because he had no idea how long he'd be out.

He called Hoyt once more from the road, but it went straight to voicemail. "For that, you brat, you're going to get a ten-inch dildo shoved up your ass."

Thirty minutes later, he pulled into a parking space at the hotel where Hoyt had been staying. The omega's truck was missing from the parking lot, so he went to the front desk to make sure Hoyt was still registered at The Black Bear Inn.

He wasn't.

Steamed, Kofi sat in the driver's seat of his car and wondered if it was ethical to ask his brother to see if he could use deputy resources to track the GPS in Hoyt's phone.

With no other ideas in mind, he went to Dak's house. Chase answered the door with Ezra in his arms.

His brother-in-law grinned. "Two weeks in a row. Dak is going to be sorry he missed you. I'd tell you to stop by the station, but he's out on a call. There's a missing hiker, and it's all-hands-on-deck for the search."

"Oh." He looked over his shoulder at the tree-covered mountains rising in the distance. "Should we be helping?"

"Not at this point, but if they don't find him soon, then they'll call for everybody in Bear's Cove to get out there." Chase stepped back. "The weather is nice, so they're not too worried. Come on in."

Kofi went into his brother's house and found himself face-to-face with Simone's beaming smile.

She sat in a ratty old chair, and knitting needles clicked in time to her rocking. "Kofi, it's so great to see you again. Did you come to take me out to lunch?"

Unsure how to answer, his gaze slid to Chase.

Chase laughed. "Grandma, don't tease. He's not as young as he used to be, and you're going to make him think his memory is shot."

"I don't mind taking the three of you to lunch." It would get his mind off his problem.

Simone got out of her chair faster than he would have thought possible. "I want to go to the baklava place."

Kofi watched her shuffle off to the rear of the house. He turned to Chase. "The baklava place?"

"Falafel Haus. It's Middle Eastern cuisine with a Dutch infusion."

"What does that taste like?"

"Garlic," Chase said, his eyes sparkling. "Lots of garlic. Dak is going to be surprised the next time we kiss."

"Or hungry."

At the restaurant, they sat at a table so Ezra's infant seat could fit. After they ordered food, Simone perched her chin on her palm, regarding Kofi thoughtfully. "You look like a young man who has lost his love."

Kofi threw another questioning glance at Chase, but Simone tapped his arm to keep his attention on her. "Sorry. I don't know what you're getting at."

"You do, too," she scoffed. "You write all those sexy romance novels. You know exactly what I'm getting at."

He understood why Dak liked Chase's great-grandmother so much. She was open and honest, and her faculties were more intact than people a quarter her age. Heat traveled up his neck. "I didn't realize you guys knew I was a writer."

"I'm a fan," Chase said. "I've been reading your books for years. When Dak caught me reading one, and he told me that his brother was the great K.F. Love, I'll admit—I was a little star struck the first time I met you."

"I like the ménage ones," Simone added. "I've had to get by with only my imagination for years."

"Grandma," Chase whispered. "I tried to set you up with the guy from the ice cream place, so don't complain."

Simone rolled her eyes. "Just because he's old doesn't mean I find him attractive." Then she returned her attention to Kofi. "Spill, honey. Tell me about the young man who is causing you so much anguish."

It would be so much easier to lie, but if he did, then any chance he had with Hoyt would evaporate. He glanced at Chase. "I'm sorry if this upsets you."

He waved away the apology. "My grandma is my best friend. We have no secrets."

"That's not what I meant." His gaze dropped, and it landed on Ezra. The baby cooed and kicked while playing with colorful trinkets attached to his seat. "It's Hoyt. We kind of hit it off last weekend, and now he won't return my calls or texts."

Chase arched one brow. "Hoyt? That's weird. Dak is convinced you hated Hoyt. I know you told him you didn't, but he said years of watching your behavior backs up his interpretation."

The server came with their meals. Kofi poked at the pita, and some tzatziki sauce spilled out through a split in the top. Avoiding someone because you wanted to cage them against a wall and kiss them senseless wasn't the same as avoiding someone because they got on your nerves.

"It's good. I promise." Chase bit into his falafel wrap.

Simone picked at her baked falafel. She'd already ordered a variety platter of baklava for dessert. "You've liked him all these years?"

Kofi started. That woman was too intuitive by half. "Yeah. I guess so."

"What did you do to upset him?" Simone shoved a huge forkful into her mouth after she lobbed that question.

Kofi wasn't sure if he bristled because she'd assumed he was at fault or from the guilt he felt over the way he'd treated Hoyt. "I told him it was just one time because it would be awkward and weird."

He shot a guilty glance in Chase's direction to find the omega watching him thoughtfully. "You really don't want to discuss this with us."

"Not really. No." He took a bite of his wrap, and he realized Chase was right—the food was very good.

Taking him at his word, Simone chatted with him for the rest of the meal, seeming to let go of the topic now that she understood the problem. They talked about places they'd both visited, comparing how they'd changed or stayed the same in the years between their visits. Chase jumped in with questions, but he mostly listened to their tales of places he'd never been.

At the end of the meal, Kofi paid the bill. While they waited for the server to return with his credit card, Chase leaned in.

"You know, I don't think Dak would care if you dated Hoyt. It might be weird at first, but I think that'll fade quickly."

The omega meant well, but he didn't understand the problem his alpha faced. "I agree he probably won't care if I date him. He'll care if bringing him around upsets you."

"Oh." Color drained from Chase's face. "Oh, don't let me stand in the way of you being happy. Hoyt and I got off on the wrong foot, but we're okay now. We went out to lunch last week. He's fun."

Simone patted Kofi's other hand. "I liked him, too. He doesn't seem at all compatible with Dak. I don't know you well enough to know whether it'll work out."

It could work out because he was committed to it and his bear demanded possession of the omega. Plus he loved Hoyt's enthusiasm and energy, two things his brother had never quite appreciated.

But nothing was going to get started if he couldn't track Hoyt down. "I need to find him."

"He went home to pack up his stuff because he's moving here next week. He's renting a place near where he's leasing for the coffee shop."

Kofi didn't know where Hoyt lived, but he was glad to hear he'd signed the lease he'd most wanted. "How do you know that?"

Chase's lips quirked with a sly smile. "I've been texting him throughout lunch. I didn't mention you. I just asked how he was and when he was coming back."

"Maybe I should wait for him to come back?"

Simone clucked her tongue. She got up and threw her thin arms around him. "Courage, now. He's already skittish. He needs to know you're committed."

His bag was already packed, so he nodded. "Chase, text me that address."

The location wasn't far from the Forrest Hills home where Kofi and his brothers had grown up. He cruised past the house that had been occupied by his fathers until they'd both perished from a foodborne illness.

Three kids ran around the front yard, playing some kind of tag, and one of their parents, in bear form, looked on. Kofi smiled as he remembered hundreds of days with his brothers spent the same way.

His brain fast-forwarded to a day when it would be his and Hoyt's kids tumbling through a yard in Bear's Cove—because that's where Hoyt's heart was set on settling. Ten minutes later, he pulled into a townhouse complex where one of his best friends had grown up.

As he parked, a man hailed him from the sidewalk. Kofi recognized his friend's father. He hopped from the car and waved. "Hi, Mr. Young. How are you?"

"I'm well. What brings you to these parts?"

"A friend of mine lives here." Kofi didn't want to spend a lot of time on pleasantries. He needed to get to Hoyt, to convince him to take a chance on something deeper, before his bear asserted itself. He retrieved his bag from the backseat and slung it over his shoulder. "It's good to see you. Tell Brandt I said hello, and give Mrs. Young my best."

With purposeful steps, he strode up the walk that led to Hoyt's townhouse.

The door opened before he got there. Hoyt stepped onto the narrow cement pad meant to be a porch. The waning evening sunlight glinted from his ginger locks, painting them with strands of gold. His skin wasn't as pale as it had been a week ago, and the tanned skin brought out the freckles sprinkled over his face and down his arms.

Kofi's breath caught at the handsomeness of his intended omega.

He turned to lock the front door, and Kofi realized Hoyt hadn't seen him.

"Hoyt."

Hoyt froze. A moment later, he finished turning the key, and the deadbolt slid into place. He hopped down the stairs without acknowledging Kofi.

Perhaps the omega hadn't heard him, and he'd frozen in thought? Or maybe Kofi had imagined it. Hoyt's gaze was pointed firmly at the ground, and his attention seemed to be on the package he carried under one arm.

Kofi moved to block Hoyt's path. "Hey."

Now Hoyt's gaze lifted. No flash of recognition or fond remembrance flickered in his crystal blue eyes. He sidestepped Kofi. "Excuse me."

This was ridiculous. Kofi wasn't going to let Hoyt get away with playing games like this. His hand shot out and wrapped around the omega's upper arm. "I know you heard me."

Hoyt's chest lifted with a deep inhale, and then he exhaled. "We concluded our business. We can go back to being polite to each other when necessary."

This was the diva temper Dak had warned him about. The reality of it didn't bother him, but the fact that he'd hurt Hoyt did. "I drove all the way out here to talk to you."

A false smile frosted Hoyt's face, and his eyes shot crystal daggers. "You should have called first. I would have told you I already have plans for tonight."

Plans? His gaze roved up and down Hoyt, noting the time and care he'd taken with his appearance. Fucker better not have a date. Kofi would disable any alpha who tried to lay a hand on Hoyt. He tamped down the rush of jealousy and focused on the moment. "I did call, but you didn't pick up or call back. I've texted too, but you haven't responded to a single one."

Not a muscle in Hoyt's face changed. "Bad cell signals out here. Excuse me. I really need to get going."

"Where?" Perhaps he didn't have a right to ask that question, but he wasn't going to back down. Simone's advice rang through his ears—Hoyt needed to know that Kofi cared.

"I'm meeting friends in the park."

Kofi pursed his lips. He needed to give Hoyt time to get over his pique so that he'd listen to what Kofi had to say. "I'll come with you."

Hoyt jerked his arm, breaking Kofi's hold. "Omegas only."

Recalling that Hoyt had been getting together with his omega friends regularly for years, Kofi backed off. "Give me your keys. I'll wait at your place."

Laughter barked from Hoyt. "Ahh, no. You're not my alpha. You have no claim to me. Go back to Matunus Bay and write your next bear shifter porn novel."

Kofi blinked. "Does everybody know about that?"

"You thought it was a secret?" Hoyt laughed again. "Ashwin showed us your books years ago. You've got the entire world thinking we're fiction and that we go around hooking up with random guys. I used to think you were a genius, but now I think you're a coward who lives in his own little made-up world. It's sad."

Obviously the secret was out. He needed to let that—and Hoyt's dig—go and focus on winning Hoyt's heart. "Look, I know you're upset, but be reasonable, okay? I just want to talk to you."

A second of hesitation, and a hint of longing broke through the icy exterior Hoyt had affected. Then it was gone, his shield firmly back in place. "Well, I don't want to talk to you."

Hoyt squared his shoulders, threw his head back, and strolled to his truck.

Watching his would-be lover leave, Kofi scrambled for another plan. Hoyt was supposed to be happy to see him. He was supposed to invite Kofi in, hear out his apology, and welcome him with arms wide open.

The opposite had happened.

Hands in pockets, he watched as Hoyt's truck carried him from the parking lot and down the street.

If Hoyt thought he'd won this, he was sorely mistaken. Kofi was far from finished.

Back when Dak had been wed to Hoyt, Kofi had timed his visits for nights when Hoyt would be out. Once each month, the omegas got together at the park for a bonfire. Dak said the omegas spent the evening roasting marshmallows, drinking, and gossiping. He used to go pick Hoyt up at the end of the night to drive him home.

Tonight, that would be Kofi's job.

He parked in the empty maintenance lot a mile from the park and watched as cars full of omegas poured into the park. When the sun had set, Kofi removed his clothes and shifted into bear form to he could blend in with the shadows. He had no intention of crashing Hoyt's party, but the omega was in a reckless mood, and he owed it to Hoyt to watch out for him.

Chapter 5—Hoyt

Flames rose to the sky, or at least that's how it appeared to Hoyt as he lay, sprawled on his back, a few feet away from the bonfire.

"Whatcha doing?" Gideon, an omega Hoyt had known since high school, plopped down on the log next to him.

"Watching the fire." The strange dance of the flames burned with different colors that were somehow wildly fascinating. The ethereal rhythms kept his mind from fixating on the man who'd appeared in front of his house. Fire had burned in his eyes as well, but it was mostly in shades of blue.

Gideon chuckled. "You're laying on the ground. How drunk are you?"

Hoyt was fairly toasted, the alcohol lending more warmth to his blood than the fire. "Drunk enough." He rolled, pushing against the ground in an attempt to sit.

Gideon grabbed his hand and tugged. His equilibrium was off-kilter as well, so the pair of them ended up stumbling around. The world teetered, and Hoyt didn't possess enough of his faculties to know which way was up.

A bear zipped by going so fast he was nothing more than a blur. It bumped into them both, sending them careening over the log and into the cooler grass away from the bonfire.

Hoyt landed on top of Gideon.

Gideon stared, his eyes wide.

"What the fuck just happened?" Hoyt felt Gideon's heartbeat against his chest, a rumble of thunder meshing with the pop and crackle of the fire.

"We lost our balance. A shifter pushed us away from the fire. He saved our lives." Gideon clutched at Hoyt, his hands wending around Hoyt's neck.

The next thing he knew, Gideon's lips mashed into his, opening hungrily to deepen the kiss.

Omegas fooled around with one another. It was a common occurrence among unmated bears, though it had been years since Hoyt had engaged in such play. He might be currently unattached, but news of his divorce had been greeted by skepticism and distrust. Some omegas thought he was stupid for ending a relationship with a Freeman, a clan of shifters known for producing alphas who were caring and loyal. Others thought he might try to go after their alphas next. Some of the unmated ones, like Gideon, had extended sympathy.

A haze of alcohol clouded his brain, and he didn't react. He didn't want to kiss Gideon, but it took a minute to process what was happening. When he did, he broke the kiss and stumbled to his feet. "I have to take a leak."

He headed toward the woods in search of a tree to provide a modicum of privacy. In the midst of relieving himself, someone bumped into him from behind.

"I didn't mean to freak you out." Gideon sagged against a nearby tree and faced away from Hoyt.

"It's fine." The kiss had felt all wrong, and it banished the haze long enough for Hoyt to recall how sinfully right Kofi's lips had felt on his. That was the bear's kiss he wanted.

He finished his task and zipped his pants. He turned to find Gideon watching him, a drunken heat in his eyes. "You have a nice ass."

This wasn't a road Hoyt wanted to travel. Tonight was meant for drinking until he forgot who Kofi was. "You're drunk."

Gideon shrugged. "So are you." He came closer. "Look, we're both single right now, and it's that kind of night. What would you say to a quick hook-up?"

Before he'd married Dak, he would have consented. But there was something about having an alpha that ruined him for any kind of sexy fun with an omega. "Thanks, but not tonight."

He went to brush past Gideon, but the omega grabbed his arm. Gideon was large for an omega. There was a time when they'd thought he might develop into an alpha, but he hadn't. "Are you sure? We can keep it between us."

"He's sure."

Hoyt whirled at the sound of the voice that haunted his dreams, and he found himself face-to-face with those deep blue eyes. Shadows shrouded Kofi's body, but Hoyt suspected he was naked underneath the lack of light. "Fuck," he muttered. "You're not supposed to be here."

Kofi's shoulder lifted, which was a decisive gesture on an alpha that told him to seek acceptance of what he couldn't change. "Let's get your things. I'm taking you home."

That sounded nice, but Hoyt remembered—with crystal clarity—why he was mad at Kofi. "I'm not going home with you."

Something flashed in Kofi's eyes and manifested in the firmness of his lips as they pressed together. "Don't test me, omega."

Gideon, bless his heart, stepped in front of Hoyt. "He doesn't belong to you anymore." The second omega leaned forward and squinted in the dim light. "Hey. You're not Dak."

"Gideon, is it?"

"Yeah. That's me." Gideon stumbled backward into Hoyt, and the two of them crashed to the forest floor with Gideon landing on top of Hoyt.

The pair broke out in peals of laughter. Gideon's weight was lifted from him, and then Hoyt found himself on his feet. Kofi's face floated inches above his.

"I won't tell you again to get your things."

A note of finality sent an apprehensive shiver through Hoyt. In a daze, he went back to the bonfire and shoved his empty beer bottles and leftover marshmallows into his bag.

Gideon touched his shoulder. "You don't have to go with him. It's forbidden for an alpha to force an omega to do things he doesn't want to do."

But Hoyt did want to go with Kofi. He'd wanted to answer his calls and respond to his texts, but he hadn't because every time he thought of Kofi, he relived the devastating blow he'd suffered when the alpha had walked out on him.

"He won't hurt me," Hoyt said. "I'm wasted, so he just wants to take me home. I'll be fine."

Gideon turned him so they were face-to-face. He clasped both of Hoyt's shoulders. "You're safe here with us. We won't let anything happen to you."

Before Hoyt could formulate a response, the world spun. Vaguely he was aware of being carried in strong arms. Then he felt the rhythm of tires moving underneath, and he knew he was in a car.

Kofi had followed through on his promise to take Hoyt home.

Thoughts whirled around Hoyt's head, most of them grievances he had against Kofi. Others consisted of conflicted feelings he had about the enigmatic alpha. Then he thought about how he could use someone to talk to about all of this.

"You know what I miss about Dak?"

"The sex." Kofi's quiet response came from the driver's seat.

Hoyt turned his head and tried to focus his bleary vision on Kofi. "No. Not that. I mean, it wasn't bad, but it wasn't like, earth-shattering or anything."

Kofi grunted.

Hoyt plowed through any noises his would-be alpha made. "I miss having a friend I could count on for anything. We fought like crazy, mostly over stupid stuff, and our relationship was a clusterfuck of a mess, but anytime I had a problem, he listened. Didn't matter what other shit was going on between us. He cared about me. I miss that."

"I care about you." Kofi's voice came out strange, strangled and low.

"You wanna fuck me," he scoffed. "Just like every other freaking alpha out there."

"I want more than just sex from you, Hoyt. I want a relationship."

"You're a fucking liar."

The rest of the ride was silent. Hoyt vaguely remembered entering his house, and he woke up alone in his bed.

With a groan, he rose. The groan wasn't due to a hangover. Hoyt wasn't the kind of person who suffered from headaches. But the morning after he'd been out drinking, it wasn't easy to wake up. He shuffled into the bathroom and performed his morning ablutions. He hadn't slept all that late, which was great because he had to finish packing up his possessions for the move to Bear's Cove. The apartment he planned to rent would be available in two days. He wanted to move right in and get to work on the renovations he'd need to do to the retail space in order to open his coffee shop. He'd taken Kofi's advice and changed the name to Perfect Blend. That hit the coffee and the matchmaking buttons.

In the kitchen, he found Kofi seated at the table and reading a newspaper. Vague memories surfaced—a bear knocking him down, Kofi driving him home.

Hoyt turned on the faucet and filled the coffee maker with water. "That's not my newspaper."

"I know. You don't follow the news." Kofi folded the section he'd been reading and set it on the table. "I went out and got it this morning." He motioned to a cardboard box on the counter. "I also picked up a couple muffins and a bear claw for you."

Bear claws were Hoyt's favorite donut shape. The bakery in town made them with a cinnamon glaze that stroked his sweet tooth in all the right ways. However he didn't want to accept gifts from Kofi.

"Of course, if you don't want the bear claw, I'll eat it. I never turn down a donut." He flashed a smile. "Maybe you're too hungover for rich food right now?"

"I'm fine." Really? Kofi was going to challenge him by threatening to eat the donut? He sounded like he actually wouldn't mind eating the pastry just to spite Hoyt. Bastard. Two could play at that game. When the coffee was ready, he poured himself a mug, plated a donut and a muffin, and he sat across from Kofi.

A small smile lifted the corners of Kofi's mouth, reminding Hoyt of exactly how kissable those lips were.

The surge of unwanted desire made him grouchy. "I don't know why you're still here. I didn't invite you in, and I didn't invite you to stay the night."

Rather than rise to the bait, Kofi toasted him with his mug. "You're welcome for the bear claw."

Hoyt's lower lip stuck out, but it was hard to keep it there while eating sugary goodness, so he abandoned the attempt to pout. He did his best to ignore Kofi while he ate. No matter where he stared, Kofi was in his peripheral vision. It was annoying and kind of awesome at the same time.

"You're going to have to talk to me sooner or later."

Hoyt sipped his coffee. "It's interesting that you think so."

"Interesting? How so?"

Fuck. Had he opened up a conduit for dialogue? He needed to shut that shit down. He shoved the rest of the bear claw in his mouth, wiped his hands on his napkin, and got up from the table. He took his mug to the sink and rinsed it.

"When are you moving?" The voice came from over Hoyt's shoulder. Kofi had followed him to the sink, and the man moved like a Ninja. Guys that big shouldn't be able to move so stealthily.

Hoyt sighed. "If I have sex with you, will you leave me alone?"

"No. I didn't come here to have sex with you."

More than willing to call Kofi's bluff on this, Hoyt pressed his ass back, rubbing it against the bulge in Kofi's jeans. To drive home his point, he let his bear whine for the alpha.

Behind him, Kofi inhaled a ragged breath.

Hoyt whimpered again, and this time he reached back to stroke the alpha's cock. "Oh, Daddy, you're so hard."

Kofi responded with a growl. His hand cupped the front of Hoyt's throat, and his nails morphed to bear claws. "Omega, you're playing with fire."

There was nothing the man could say, so he let his bear do the talking. Resting his back against Kofi's chest, he let out a series of submissive whines. These were rare sounds, designed to arouse an alpha's dominant sexual tendencies. Hoyt was playing a dangerous game, but he was more than willing to accept the consequences of manipulating an alpha. He wanted Kofi to possess him once more before they permanently parted ways.

The claws at his throat traced the barest path, scratching lightly over Hoyt's sensitive skin as they traveled lower. A low growl, originating so deeply it vibrated almost near the base of Hoyt's spine, rumbled through Kofi.

Kofi's hands stroked Hoyt's body. Confident and knowing, they found the places that elicited moans and urged plaintive whimpers. Soon Hoyt found himself shirtless with his pants tangled around his ankles. A bed might be more comfortable, but he'd aroused the bear, and now he had to deal with Kofi's primal nature. This wouldn't be a romantic interlude. Hoyt hadn't wanted that anyway.

He heard Kofi's zipper unknit, and he reached for the bottle of olive oil he kept in a nearby cupboard. Thank goodness he hadn't finished packing the kitchen yet.

Kofi held out a hand, and Hoyt poured a good amount of oil into his palm. The alpha coated his cock, and then he massaged the lubricant into Hoyt's sphincter. Fingers penetrated next, and Hoyt found himself breathing heavy at the fingers sawing in and out of his ass. He moaned, and the alpha growled his approval.

The tip of Kofi's wide cock nudged his entrance. The dominant bear was taller and larger, and he pushed Hoyt forward, forcing him to bend over the sink. Kofi's cock slid into his ass, a throbbing and insistent reminder that he was in charge.

Wasting no time, Kofi fucked Hoyt. He pounded into the omega's body, claiming and possessing it with each powerful thrust. His claws raked down Hoyt's back and across his front, an unrelenting sensation that sent rivulets of pleasure winding through Hoyt's body. He'd never felt like this before. No alpha had owned him as much as Kofi in those moments. Later it might scare Hoyt, but right now he was too far gone to care.

Soon Kofi reached around, and his hand closed over Hoyt's neglected cock. Their movements became frenzied. Tension coiled tighter, and an orgasm detonated. Hoyt's semen shot into the sink, and it dribbled onto Kofi's hand. With a mighty roar, the alpha climaxed. His hot spunk filled Hoyt, spreading a different kind of pleasure to his insides.

Kofi slumped forward, his weight bearing down on Hoyt. His arms banded about the omega, holding him as they both trembled. "Hoyt, my omega." Kofi's words were a whispered caress as his breath rushed across Hoyt's neck, making him shiver.

After a time, Kofi's softened cock slipped from him, and the alpha turned him around. His lips crashed into Hoyt's, demanding a kiss as his due. Already bereft of his senses, Hoyt submitted to the onslaught. He luxuriated in the harshness of this affection, and the feel of Kofi's claws moving over his exposed skin only compounded the sense of belonging.

The kiss broke, and Kofi's lips moved down Hoyt's neck in sucking bites that each left a mark. Then, without warning, sharp bear teeth penetrated his shoulder.

Hoyt cried out, jerking in Kofi's arms, but the alpha had him pinned in place. He breathed through the pain. The teeth retracted, morphing back to human teeth, but the pain remained.

Kofi's finger moved softly over the mark. "My omega, you can't move when your alpha is marking you."

That warning acted like icy water to his face. Hoyt broke free of Kofi's hold. He pulled his pants up and snatched his shirt from the counter. He glowered at Kofi. "You're not my alpha, and I'm not your omega. We fucked. That's all. The door is that way." He flung his arm out, pointing to the front of the townhouse.

Kofi didn't move, so Hoyt marched into the living room. A black nylon bag was on the sofa. It wasn't his, so he assumed it was Kofi's. He picked it up, and something metal clanked inside.

Standing in the threshold to the kitchen, Kofi frowned. He'd fixed his clothes. "Hoyt, I came here to talk to you. I wanted to apologize for how I left things last time."

Fury burned in Hoyt's chest, and it had roots in a hurt he didn't want to face. He'd fallen in love with Kofi years ago. The realization left him shaken, full of guilt and shame. This shifter didn't love him back. The sex had been great—earth-shattering, if he wanted to be honest—and he'd come back for more. Their unique circumstances left Kofi unable to be the alpha Hoyt needed—one who put him first. Kofi would never do that because Hoyt had been married to Dak.

"Apology accepted." Anything to get him to leave. Hoyt wanted to bury his face in his pillow and sob. "Mission accomplished. You can sleep well at night knowing I'm not harboring a grudge."

A muscle ticked on Kofi's jaw, and he crossed his arms. The move emphasized his upper body muscles and made Hoyt want to touch and lick. But the ire in the alpha's steely gaze forbade contact. "I know you're upset, but that tone is unnecessary. I mean it, Hoyt—I want to take a chance on us."

A week ago, Hoyt had been more than prepared to weather the storm a relationship between them might spawn. He'd been eager to make peace with Dak and Chase. He'd even mentally prepared conversation starters for when he saw Ashwin and Cruz, the other two Freeman brothers.

But Kofi hadn't been. He'd made it abundantly clear Hoyt meant nothing to him. There was no coming back from that.

He shoved the bag toward Kofi. "Well, I don't."

"Hoyt, please. I came here to see you, talk to you—show you that I want more."

The rattling in the bag belied Kofi's intentions. Hoyt knew exactly what the alpha had packed—kinky sex gear. He unzipped the bag and pulled out a flogger and handcuffs. "You came here to fuck me. You did that. Now leave."

Faced with such stark evidence, Kofi shook his head. "Maybe I was hopeful we'd get there, but it wasn't why I came. I need you, Hoyt. I—I have feelings for you, and I know you have feelings for me."

Feelings? Fuck that. It wasn't enough. Nothing Kofi could say or do would erase the heartache and hurt he'd dealt Hoyt. "It's too late. I'm over you." Then he gave Kofi a pointed look. "We had a nice time today, Kofi. I don't regret what's happened between us. Now, I have things to do, so please leave."

Chapter 6—Kofi

Having his own words thrown back in his face caught Kofi by surprise. He'd been in relationships with omegas before, and he was used to them behaving submissively—especially after sex. He'd never bitten an omega before. The ancient display was a bonding ritual that subdued an omega, rendering them docile. At least, it was supposed to.

Hoyt was feisty as hell, which he liked, but right now it was driving him past the bounds of an alpha's patience.

He took the bag Hoyt had dropped at his feet, and he nailed the omega with a firm look. "I'll go, but once you've calmed down and moved past your anger, I want you to think about what I'm offering and what you truly need in your life to be happy and fulfilled."

Inside the quiet sanctity of his car, he waited for Hoyt to come after him. Minutes passed, and nothing happened.

Eventually he started the engine and drove away. The miles between Forrest Hills and Bear's Cove were connected by a two-lane highway that wound through forests and over mountainous terrain. He called Dak, putting his brother on speaker.

"Kofi, how are you?" Dak's voice boomed through the car's audio system.

"Not as well as I'd hoped."

"Chase told me about your conversation with him. I take it your plan didn't work out."

"Nope. Not even a little bit." Something occurred to Kofi. Chase had issued assurances the day before, but he wanted to hear from his brother as well. It wasn't that he didn't trust Chase; it was that he owed his brother the respect of asking directly. "Hey—you don't mind, right?"

"I'm not going to lie and say it's not weird. I mean, for all these years, I thought you hated Hoyt, and then it turns out you had a thing for him. If I had known, I would have stepped aside years ago. We were never in love. Both of us tried to make it work for our parents' sake, but it was doomed to failure. We were not at all compatible. I didn't see it then, but I see it now." Dak cleared his throat. "I'm happy, Kofi. I'm happier than I ever thought possible, and I want that for you and Hoyt. You're both great guys, and you deserve it."

"Thanks. Your blessing means a lot to me, though I know it's going to piss off Hoyt."

Dak chuckled. "Probably. He's headstrong and stubborn, which are his best and worst qualities. Once he makes up his mind, nothing's going to change it."

Kofi scrubbed a hand through his hair. "He's decided he doesn't want anything to do with me."

"Why not? Maybe I misread you when I thought you didn't like him, but I know I didn't misread him. He's had a crush on you the whole time we were married. Why do you think I never urged you two to bond? He used to hang out with Ashwin and Cruz fairly often."

This was news to Kofi. He'd spent the last seven years on a self-induced exile from his home to he could avoid causing heartache for his youngest brother. "We hooked up last weekend when I went over to read contracts, but then I blew him off because I wasn't sure how you would react."

"Oh. That's unfortunate." Dak sighed. "He's the most stubborn person I've ever dealt with, but he usually comes around if he's in the wrong. If you're serious about him, don't give up—give him time."

His brother's solution would require patience, and Kofi wasn't sure he had the endurance. "He's had a week away from me, and it has only cemented in his head that he wants nothing to do with me."

"Don't stay away from him. Just don't pressure him. He's moving to Bear's Cove, which is closer to Matunus Bay. Stop by his shop to see how it's going. Send chocolate or a honey-baked ham. Be a presence in his life. Let him see you're not going anywhere."

He could do that, though it would be easier if he had an apartment in Bear's Cove. "Okay. You just went through the real estate search process. Can you recommend any rental properties in Bear's Cove?"

"If you're serious, buy a house. Hoyt will use any excuse to put you off. I'll text you contact information for my realtor."

Staying in Dak's guest room while he waited to sign on a property was kind of fun. This living arrangement came with access to his nephew, and as a bonus, Simone adopted him as a grandson.

Kofi found himself writing less because he couldn't get enough of little Ezra, and spending time with the baby made him yearn for one of his own.

"Hoyt is at the shop right now. He said he's trying to figure out how to decorate it." Chase poured coffee into a travel mug. "I'm going to stop by to help him with a dishwasher that doesn't work."

"Oh?" Kofi bounced Ezra on his knee and made a face that set off peals of laughter from the infant.

A sly smile grew on Chase's face. "Want to come with me? I'm going to need someone to watch Ezra while I'm fixing the dishwasher."

Kofi had yet to find the courage to happen by Hoyt's shop. The omega had signed a lease on the shop he'd wanted, which was the one Kofi had suggested was better in terms of the location and the lease price. It had an option to buy, which Kofi felt was important.

"Sure." He managed to sound more confident than he felt.

They loaded themselves and little Ezra into the van with all of Chase's repair equipment. When they arrived, Chase handed Kofi a cloth contraption with straps attached. "It's Dak's, so it'll fit you."

He accepted the thing, though he had no idea what it was. "You want me to wear this?"

"It's a baby sling. Ezra isn't heavy, but carrying him around for a couple hours can make him seem like he's ten times his actual size."

Kofi held it up, trying to discern what went where. "I see."

With a laugh, Chase snatched it away, and he fit the sling to Kofi's torso. Then he stuck Ezra inside. The baby faced out so he could see the world.

"If he gets tired, you can turn him around to face you, and then he can snuggle into you and fall asleep." Chase handed over a backpack. "Bottles and diapers."

"Diapers?" This idea alarmed Kofi. "I'm not qualified for that."

Chase hefted his toolbox. "I have every confidence you'll figure it out." The omega's sly smile sidled to the storefront and back. "It's an enviable skill that too few alphas possess."

Kofi felt like he was being played, but he didn't care. "Do you want me to meet you back here in a couple hours?"

"Yes, but I want you to walk me inside, and then ask."

The door to the empty storefront was unlocked. The building had room for three businesses, but two of the spaces—Hoyt's included—were empty. On the far end was a fitness center. Shifters came and went, each carrying water bottles, and some had bags for soiled clothing or towels.

He followed Chase inside and looked around. The interior was not nearly ready to open. Though the walls had been painted and the flooring was new, there was no sales counter or furniture of any kind.

"Chase?" Hoyt's voice called from a room in the back.

"None other." Chase winked at Kofi. "I brought Ezra."

Hoyt sailed through a threshold and into the vast, open space. The brilliant smile on his face froze when he saw Kofi.

Spying Hoyt, Ezra shrieked with excitement, kicking his feet and waving his arms.

Kofi indicated the excited infant. "Do you want to hold him?"

Indecision had Hoyt biting his lip in an adorable way that made Kofi want to lick away the sting.

He lifted Ezra out of the sling and held him out. "Come on. I promise I won't bite unless you ask nicely."

A blush traveled up Hoyt's pale neck, suffusing his face with a color Kofi had grown to love. The omega swallowed, making his Adam's apple bob. He approached on feet that trudged through molasses.

Chase set down his toolbox. The clunk of metal on wood echoed through the air, and Hoyt flinched.

Kofi hadn't intended to make Hoyt jumpy. He'd wanted him off-kilter, but he hadn't wanted the omega to be fearful. He put effort into softening his expression as he handed over the kid. "He's excited to see you."

Ezra laughed and lunged the rest of the way into Hoyt's arms. The omega smiled and hugged the child to his chest.

It struck Kofi that this could soon be their life—coming into Hoyt's store and handing over their infant son. But first he had to wait out the stubborn man's refusal to have anything to do with him.

He parked his hands on his hips and looked around. "This is a nice amount of space for your shop, and the location is great. You could do health drinks as well because there's a fitness place on the other end of the building." He pointed out the side bank of windows. "You should see about putting a patio out there, where it's visible from the beach."

Hoyt turned away from Kofi, facing Chase while keeping his attention focused on Ezra. He grinned at the infant and spoke in a sing-song tone that held Ezra spellbound. "Thank you for coming. I tried to fix it, but I might have made it worse."

Chase motioned to the back room. "Show me."

Kofi moved closer to Hoyt and held out his arms to take his nephew back. "I'm babysitting while you two fix stuff."

"Oh." Hoyt bounced Ezra on his hip. "I wondered why you were here."

Swooping closer while wearing his sexiest grin, Kofi brushed his arm against Hoyt's chest as he took possession of the child. Hoyt's scent set off alarm bells inside Kofi, only he wasn't sure why. He didn't smell like he'd been with another alpha, but something was off. While he tried to pinpoint it, he responded to Hoyt's statement. "I'm moving to Bear's Cove, so you'll probably see me around a lot."

Hoyt's jaw dropped, but the news didn't silence him. "You're moving here? Seriously? What an original idea. Wait—did you get Dak's permission first? Because he might be mad that you decided to start over in a new place where he happens to be."

Goodness, but the sarcastic tone in Hoyt's voice brought to mind visions of turning the hot little ginger over his knee and turning his ass the color of his hair. Suppressing the urge, he grinned. "Thank you for your concern. I did discuss it with Dak first. He was the one who suggested it was time to put down roots, and I'm staying with him while I wait to sign the papers on a house I'm buying."

"Well." Hoyt parked his hands on his hips and shot lasers at Kofi. "That's awfully convenient. Don't think I want you coming around here, because I don't."

He'd expected the omega to be ornery, so he was prepared. Placing his hand to his heart, he sighed. "And here I thought you'd appreciate my business. A writer needs a coffeehouse with good wireless internet and tasty snacks. This is necessary fuel for productive creativity."

"Whatever." Hoyt rolled his eyes and motioned to Chase. "Let's get to that dishwasher. And next time, if you need someone to watch Ezra while you work, I'm perfectly happy to do it."

Ignoring Hoyt's graceless dismissal, Kofi situated Ezra in his sling. "Let's go for a walk, E. I want to show you where I'm moving."

The house he'd purchased was large, and it was in walking distance to Hoyt's place of business. This was by design. Should things progress the way he wanted with his intended mate, then the location would be convenient. If not—fuck that—he wasn't going to consider the possibility of failure.

A little over an hour later, Chase texted to say he was almost finished. Ezra had enjoyed the walk; the entire time, he'd seemed to be excited about both the conversation and the view. His little arms waved, and he laughed and chattered. One day, Kofi hoped to give him a cousin with a similar rosy outlook on life.

Upon returning to the shop, he found Hoyt staring at a wall and frowning. The alpha part of his nature wanted to fix whatever was wrong. He approached the omega, noting how Hoyt's breathing sped up. Needing physical contact, he touched Hoyt's arm lightly. That scent was back, and it combined with the light touch. A zing went through him, a realization of something deeper and more meaningful—his intended mate was breeding. That was the scent he'd caught earlier. His alpha nature rose up and cheered, and a million questions livestreamed through his head.

The most important was this: Did Hoyt know he was pregnant?

If he did know, when did he plan to tell Kofi?

Forcing himself to stay in the moment, Kofi focused on finding the cause of Hoyt's frown. "What's wrong?"

"Nothing's wrong. I'm picking out furniture."

Kofi looked at the selection on Hoyt's phone. "You're trying to decide whether you want booths or tables?"

"I kind of wanted to do a little of both." He motioned to the inside wall. "Booths over there, and tables for the rest of the place." Hoyt exhaled hard, and a small whine escaped.

His instincts kicked in, responding to the omega's bear side. Kofi inched closer, and he set his hand on the small of Hoyt's back. "What about a few high-top tables? You could put them over next to the windows where there's a partial view of the ocean."

Fighting the primal pull between them, Hoyt's whole body shuddered.

Kofi wanted to put his arm around the omega, draw him closer, and assure him all would be fine, but he didn't have that right. Yet. Taking pity on Hoyt, he put a few inches between them. "When are you ordering the furniture?"

"Right now. It's going to take me forever to get it all set up in time for opening day." He glanced toward the front window where a sign advertised they'd be open for business in two short weeks.

"Let us know when it's going to be delivered. We'll help get it set up."

Hoyt shook his head. "That's not necessary."

Pretending the continued rejection didn't sting, Kofi shrugged. "Suit yourself. Chase texted me that he was almost ready. I'm going to head back and see if he needs help finishing up. Can you take Ezra for a few minutes?"

He hadn't missed the joy on Hoyt's face when he'd held the infant earlier, though now he wondered if it had something to do with the paternal hormones that had to be coursing through Hoyt's blood.

Without waiting for Hoyt to respond, he unhooked the main strap securing the baby sling and handed Ezra to Hoyt.

"Thanks."

Noting the return of wonder to Hoyt's face, he went into the kitchen where he found Chase under a cabinet.

"We're back. Ezra is out front with Hoyt. How did things go here?"

A grunt came from inside the cabinet. "Well enough. The dishwasher came with the place. He's either going to have to replace it within a year or spend a lot of money on replacement parts." Due to the metal surrounding him, Chase's voice echoed flatly. He backed out of the cabinet and knelt up, a grin on his face. "How was your walk?"

"We had fun. I showed Ezra the house I'm buying. He approved. He also likes to watch sea critters skittering around on the rocks. We had a long talk about insects, crabs, and other life lessons."

Chase glanced around and got to his feet. "Hoyt has been a mess since you left. I don't think I've ever seen him so nervous. Every time he started to say something, he'd stop and go in the other room."

Did that mean Hoyt wanted to confide in Chase, but he didn't trust the omega to keep his confidence? Kofi wanted Hoyt to make friends in Bear's Cove. He needed to feel like this was his home, and it was easiest to do that when family and friends were nearby.

"Chase, maybe you should ask Hoyt to hang with you and some of your omega friends."

In the midst of packing his tools, Chase snorted. "You're funny. I'm an outcast in these parts. The only friend I had moved to the middle of nowhere because he fell in love with a Warden. My alpha is my best friend. Other than that, I'm only really accepted by his friends and co-workers. Sure, people are nice enough to me, and they'll hire me to fix whatever is broken, but they don't really want to associate with someone who is half human."

Kofi stared uncomprehendingly. He'd spent the past seven years living amongst humans—who either didn't believe shifters were real or who thought shifters were freaks of nature. It had been hell having to hide his shifter side or go long stretches of time without being able to shift. But that had been his choice. He couldn't imagine living here, in a place that was supposed to be a sanctuary, and not be accepted.

He didn't quite know what to say that would make Chase feel better. After all, what reason could he give that would make it okay to accept being marginalized for being born a certain way? None.

A pipe wrench lay on the floor near where Chase had been working. Kofi scooped it up and handed it over. "So maybe then you might invite him to hang out because he's new in town, and you could use a friend?"

Chase flashed a grin, showcasing a bit of the party boy he'd left behind. "Maybe. It would be nice to hang out with someone not connected to Dak. Oh, wait." He infused just enough sarcasm so that the last part wouldn't be mistaken as a realization.

Putting a new spin on it could help. Kofi chuckled. "He's not connected anymore. One might consider that he also feels like an outcast right now."

"True." Chase secured the latch on his toolbox. "I'll think about it."

"What's holding you back?"

Chase shrugged and turned away, but Kofi snagged his arm, forcing him to halt.

"Chase, Hoyt wouldn't reject your offer of friendship because you're half human. He's not prejudiced like that."

Chase lifted a blond brow. "Then you're saying he suffers from another prejudice?"

Kofi snorted. "He doesn't like alphas who make mistakes."

A scoffing noise came from the doorway.

They both turned to find Hoyt standing with Ezra.

Kofi didn't comment. He merely held his arms out for Ezra. "We have to get going. We'll see you later. That offer of help still stands."

He made sure his arm brushed against Hoyt's during the infant-transfer process. Sparks arced between them, and a slow blush traveled up Hoyt's neck.

"Yeah," Hoyt said. "Maybe."

"Not maybe." Chase clapped Hoyt on the shoulder. "Definitely call me. I'm happy to spend a day helping a friend."

On the way out, Chase flashed an uncertain smile at Kofi, and Kofi was glad he'd encouraged Chase to seek a friendship. It would be good for both omegas.

Chapter 7—Hoyt

He couldn't fucking believe it. Kofi had followed him to Bear's Cove. Yeah, the alpha had a brother here, but he had two brothers elsewhere, and he could do his job from anywhere in the world. Why did he have to do it from here?

Hoyt threw himself into getting his place ready. He spent every waking moment there. Kofi stopped by a few times, always unexpectedly, but never alone. He came three times with Chase—that man was incredible when it came to fixing things—and he came once with Dak to pick up a tool Chase had left behind.

One look from those brilliant blue eyes peeking out from under that black mop of hair, and Hoyt felt like he'd done some strenuous cardio. It was all he could do to get his heart and breathing under control.

Even if that wasn't going on, his fucking pale skin revealed exactly how much Kofi affected him. Nobody should be that handsome or that sexy or that virile. Nobody. It should be illegal.

And his bear needed to simmer down and shut the fuck up.

Yes—Hoyt was fed up with having Kofi around. At least today, when the furniture was being delivered, he would only have to contend with Chase.

He'd gone out for coffee a few times with Dak's omega, and he found that he really liked the guy. They were as different as night and day, though they had many things in common, such as a love of good coffee and an appreciation for the same bands.

Chase had promised he wouldn't bring Dak or anyone else with him to help put together and move the furniture into place. Everything else was set and ready to go for his big opening in two days. The shelves were stocked. After the furniture was set up, he only had to come in and make food items to sell. His dream was finally coming true, and the excitement of anticipation ran rampant in his blood.

A semi-truck backed into the parking lot, and Hoyt supervised the unloading. Chase's car pulled into the lot fifteen minutes later.

The blond man jogged toward him. "Sorry I'm late. Ezra has started this phase where he cries every time I leave the room. Grandma made me leave, but I don't know. What if he needs me, and I'm letting him down?"

Hoyt didn't want Chase to abandon him, but he also didn't want to separate him from his son. "Oh. If you need to bail, I completely understand."

"It's not that." Chase sighed as he ran a hand through his hair where it was longer on top. "Grandma said it's normal to feel this way. She said he'd be fine once I left. In my heart, I know she's right. But my protective instincts are screaming at me. Ugh."

He set a hand on Chase's shoulder. "Thanks for being here, but I'll still understand if you need to slip away."

Chase's eyes lit with a merry light. "You think I'm looking for an excuse to get out of helping you. Friends don't do that. And afterward, we can go out and get beers. Dak's brothers are in town, and the four of them are hanging out, so I have the night free. Grandma already has an evening planned with Ezra."

This caught Hoyt's interest. It wasn't often Ashwin and Cruz came this far east. They'd both settled in Bear Falls, which was a gorgeous piece of heaven thousands of miles away in a warded area hidden in the Rocky Mountains.

"That's nice. I'll bet Dak is happy to see them. They haven't been out this way since their fathers passed away." A hint of bittersweetness tinged Hoyt's observation. He missed being part of a large family. No matter what had been going on between him and Dak, Ashwin and Cruz had always treated him like a brother.

"He took the rest of the week off. Kofi closed on his house this morning, so they're going to help him get it cleaned out. They want to paint and fix some stuff, and then they'll move his things out of storage and into the house." Chase grinned. "Of course, I'll be there tomorrow to change out the hot water heater and help with some other repairs. Apparently part of it has a renter, so Kofi wants to make sure all the stuff in the apartment is in working order."

That jealousy flared again. He wished the brothers would stop by and help him out, but then he scolded himself. He'd extracted a promise from Chase to come alone for a reason—he didn't trust himself around Kofi at all.

Almost as if he'd voiced the wish and his fairy godmother was hovering nearby, the door opened, and four alphas sauntered inside.

Ashwin was first. A broad grin stretched his devilishly handsome features. All four of the Freeman brothers possessed similar features. From their prominent cheekbones and square jaws to their aquiline noses, perfect eyebrows, and dark lashes, each was a feast for the eyes. To top it off, they all tended to smell really fucking good.

Though Dak and Kofi had black hair and blue eyes, Ashwin and Cruz featured rich brown, wavy locks and deep brown eyes. Cruz's were so dark, they sometimes appeared black.

"Hoyt, there you are, you ginger devil!" Ashwin picked him up and whirled him around, and then he hugged the omega tightly.

Hoyt found himself passed to Cruz before he could respond. Then he was given to Kofi who slung an arm across his shoulders. Hoyt wasn't sure if it was a friendly or a possessive arm, but he was sure the contact was both thrilling and agitating.

Ashwin and Cruz had gone on to greet Chase. The omega's eyes were wide with surprise, so Hoyt couldn't be mad at him for this trick. Obviously Chase hadn't known the Freeman alphas would show up.

Part of Hoyt wanted to move away from Kofi. Just the proximity played games with his senses. But an insistent, primal part of him wanted to burrow into Kofi's side and accept the protection he offered.

Dak spread his hands wide, and a half-smile curved his lips. "I'd apologize for showing up unexpectedly, but we're here to help you set up your shop, so I'll skip that part. We're not sorry anyway."

"Nope," Ashwin added. "Not even a little bit. Last night, when Chase said he planned to help you today, we decided to help as well. Besides, we couldn't imagine coming all this way and not seeing you."

Cruz opened up one of the long boxes. "You were right, Kofi. We're going to have to put this stuff together. It's a good thing we brought power tools."

Kofi's arm fell away from Hoyt's shoulders, and the four alphas got to work. They were loud, yelling orders across the room to one another as they took charge. Kofi and Ashwin teamed up to put a table together while Dak and Cruz tackled a set of chairs.

Chase tugged at Hoyt's wrist. "It's pointless to resist, so come help me."

With all that help, the work progressed quickly. Four hours later, all the tables and chairs were assembled. Hoyt pushed against a booth's bench seat to reposition it, and Kofi halted his action.

"What are you doing?" He shook away Kofi's hold.

A frown darkened Kofi's features. "We'll do the heavy lifting."

"It's not heavy."

Kofi leaned down, making his reply private. "Don't test me on this, omega."

The warning in his tone reverberated through Hoyt. His heart beat faster—or maybe that was because the scent of Kofi's body and the heat rolling from him affected Hoyt in ways that scrambled his better sense? He didn't know, and he couldn't seem to find the will to oppose the order.

He took a position in the center of the room and bossed around four alphas as they moved all the furniture into the positions he indicated. He felt a little mollified by the fact that Dak wouldn't let Chase do any of the heavy lifting either.

"It looks good." Chase folded his arms as he stood next to Hoyt and surveyed the setup.

"Yeah. It's exactly what I wanted."

Kofi set a hand on Hoyt's shoulder, the unexpected contact too pleasant. "Good. I'm glad we could be here to help you achieve your dream."

When he'd decided on this course for his life, Hoyt hadn't counted on anyone wanting to help him, much less the family he'd divorced. Part of him wondered why Kofi wouldn't just let him be. He'd rejected the alpha over and over and over. The rest of him sighed with contentment whenever it caught sight or scent of him. These conflicting emotions left him grumbly, and he was tired of waging this internal battle.

He wished Kofi would just let him be. Mustering the last of his energy, he resisted touching the warm, strong hand on his shoulder. "Thank you, to all of you, for helping. I hadn't planned on calling it a day this early." He had a few hours of free time. Now he would have more time to work on the next day's foodstuffs.

"Chase, let's get back to Ezra." Dak slung an arm around his omega's waist and led him out the door.

Ashwin and Cruz hugged him. "We'll be by tomorrow for coffee."

Kofi was the last one out. A crooked smile hung on his face. "I'll see you around."

After putting together ingredients for a breakfast parfait he intended to feature, Hoyt went home alone.

His rental was in a beautiful spot a ten-minute walk away. Tucked in the side of the mountain overlooking the ocean and surrounded by a lush evergreen forest, it was a seaside paradise. Hoyt's apartment was small, a loft above the garage, but he had a patio out back in the small patch of yard that belonged to him. The renters in the main house had moved out the weekend before, so he had the place pretty much to himself until the next people, probably a family or several couples, moved in for a vacation stint.

Stairs along the outside of the garage led to the second floor where he lived. He climbed the wooden risers and found an envelope taped to the outside of his door. Snatching it off, he disengaged the lock and went inside where he tore it open. His eyes scanned the page to find a notice that the property had changed hands. The new owner intended to honor the terms of the leasing agreement.

Hoyt didn't care who owned the place as long as it didn't affect him. He set the notice on top of his two-drawer filing cabinet and shucked his clothes on the way to the shower. The day had been long, and he was looking forward to throwing back a cold beer while shoveling whatever leftovers were in the fridge into his mouth.

Water sluiced over his body, washing away sweat, dirt, and stress. Afterward, he felt better, but he was still antsy. Spending the day so close to Kofi—even if he hadn't said or done anything upsetting—had been difficult.

Wearing boxer shorts and a loose cotton shirt, he headed to the kitchenette nestled in one corner of the living space. The bathroom and bedroom were the only other rooms, which suited him just fine. He opened the fridge and grabbed a beer. As he twisted off the cap, he heard the sounds of unfamiliar vehicles coming up the driveway.

Peering out the window overlooking the black asphalt, he saw two pickup trucks and a sedan.

A familiar sedan.

As he watched, Ashwin, Dak, and Cruz spilled from the trucks, and Kofi emerged from the sedan.

Realization dawned immediately. "Motherfucker bought the property I'm renting. Asshole."

His temper exploded. He slammed the open beer bottle onto the small dinette table and stormed out of the apartment. As he pounded down the stairs, he shook a finger at Kofi.

"No. You can't do this."

In the midst of unloading boxes from his trunk, Kofi paused. He faced Hoyt, his expression unreadable. "I already did."

White-hot rage slammed through Hoyt's system. "This is stalking, and it's pathetic for you to run around, following a man who has turned you down repeatedly." He poked a finger into Kofi's chest, which was equally as steely as his eyes.

Kofi wrapped his hand around Hoyt's, halting the jab of the fingertip into his chest. He leaned closer to Hoyt and spoke softly. "Fair warning—I spank omegas who forget how to show proper respect to an alpha."

Though Hoyt had more to say, Kofi's warning was enough. Yeah, he'd loved the last spanking, which was the first one he'd ever had. However, Kofi's tone guaranteed he wouldn't like the next one. He also remembered he wasn't wearing pants, just boxer shorts and a shirt.

Hoyt swallowed down his remarks, jerked his hand from Kofi's hold, and marched back up the steps.

He muttered under his breath, but he didn't say anything loud enough for Kofi to pick up on.

And yet, when he reached his apartment, he found Kofi on his heels. Hoyt opened the door, and Kofi barged through the opening before he could shut it.

"I didn't invite you in."

Kofi looked around, taking in the quaint space. Hoyt had decorated the bare walls with prints and shelves of knick-knacks. During the ten seconds it took for Kofi to respond, Hoyt hoped Kofi liked his style.

Finally Kofi closed the door. The latch clicked into place, a question rather than firm resolve. "I thought you were given a notice I had taken possession of the property."

"It didn't say who, just that there was a new owner. The note said it wouldn't change anything."

Kofi lifted his chin in a challenge. "It doesn't."

"I can't believe you followed me here, and I can't believe you bought this house. There are a million other houses for sale around here. Okay, maybe not a million, but a lot—plenty of others where I don't happen to live. You did this on purpose to get back at me."

Hoyt paused for a breath, so Kofi jumped in. "I did it on purpose, but not to get back at you. I like the house, and I'm partial to the tenant."

The admission, though not new, hit Hoyt like a bolt of lightning. Even though he'd repeatedly rejected Kofi's advances, the man wasn't giving up. Too proud to admit he was tired—he was nowhere near defeated—Hoyt thrust his shoulders back and held his head high. He most certainly ignored the heat creeping up his neck. "Well, this tenant isn't partial to you, Mr. Freeman."

The only evidence he'd scored a hit was the subtle tightening of Kofi's mouth before it curved with a sultry smile. "That becoming blush gives you away every time. One day, you're going to forget why you're mad at me, and when that day comes, I'm going to make you blissfully happy."

Promises like that heated Hoyt's blood and made his temper boil, not that it took much for Kofi to get it going. "That day is never going to come, asshole. I can't believe you're this desperate. Has no one ever turned you down? Are you having trouble taking no for an answer? You have a problem, Kofi. You need therapy. At the very least, you need to figure out what happened to your pride and self-esteem. You've turned into a pathetic excuse for a man."

While he didn't mean most of what he said, he couldn't seem to control the nastiness pouring from his mouth. More came, and he didn't pay much attention to what he said. Hoyt was wholly focused on his emotions. Topping the list was the debilitating sting of Kofi's initial rejection and the crippling humiliation that roiled through him every time he thought about it.

Next was anger. Kofi hadn't bothered to ask for time to think about it. They'd spent the day having the kind of sex Hoyt had only read about in Kofi's novels, and Kofi had walked away without a backward glance. He'd ripped out Hoyt's heart, trampled on it, and now he wanted to take it all back. That's not how these things worked.

Underneath all those complex emotions was fear. Hoyt was equally afraid that Kofi wouldn't give up and that he would concede defeat. On the one hand, if he stuck around, Hoyt would live under the constant expectation that Kofi would one day walk away. And if he left right now, it would deliver a blow from which his tender heart would not recover.

So he said horrible things because it was easier to get over someone if there hadn't been much of a relationship in the first place. He attacked Kofi's motivation, character, and his career. He trampled on the whole concept of alphas and omegas, kicking up a cloud of dirt that obscured the underlying issues, which made him feel a lot better.

Eventually he fell silent.

Through it all, Kofi had listened without interrupting, the grim set of his jaw the only indication that Hoyt's torrent of horrid words bothered him.

The silence stretched an uncomfortable length of time, and Hoyt realized he wasn't in control of the situation. Even when he'd been spewing nasty sentiments at Kofi, he hadn't been in control. This was confirmed when the alpha shattered the silence with a quiet question.

"Are you finished?"

There was nothing to do but double down. Hoyt crossed his arms and stuck out one defiant hip. "This isn't one of your fucking romance novels. This is real life."

A grim smile slashed across Kofi's face. "When an omega goes for a long period of time without the benefit of an alpha, he finds himself floundering and unhappy. You, Hoyt, are one of the least happy people I've ever come across."

"I don't need a fucking alpha. I had one for six years, and it didn't do the trick. Alphas are vastly overrated."

Kofi winced, probably because Hoyt had attacked his brother, but he responded with an even softer tone. "You had a bad match, and I'm sorry for that—for both of your sakes. But I'm here now, and you need to be taken in hand. For your tirade today, you've earned a spanking. Drop your pants and bend over the table."

Hoyt stared. "You're not fucking serious."

Both eyebrows lifted in a challenge. "You're suffering, and I'm going to ease your pain."

"By causing me more pain?"

"By showing you that you can count on me to take care of you. You need this, Hoyt. And what's more—you want it."

Kofi was too perceptive by half. Hoyt did crave the feel of Kofi's hand on him, and yet the idea of becoming dependent on Kofi left him shivering with fear—and anticipation.

Driven by a need in the core of his omega self, Hoyt found himself standing in front of the small rectangular table sitting against the wall near the kitchenette. He slid his boxer shorts down, letting them pool around his ankles. The wall was in the way, so he bent over halfway, and he braced himself with his palms on the table. If Kofi tried for more than a spanking, Hoyt would not turn him down.

Conflicting emotions ran rampant in Hoyt, which heightened all of the feelings already out of control.

Waves of warmth emanated from Kofi's body and crashed against the tsunami roiling inside Hoyt. "Do you want a gag?"

The apartment was fairly isolated. Outside, Ashwin, Dak, and Cruz called to each other as they hefted boxes and carried them into the house. They might hear him if he cried out too loudly, but Hoyt didn't care. "No."

Kofi rested his hand on the middle of Hoyt's back, the gentle weight a reminder that if he moved, Kofi was strong enough to hold him down. This tender show of dominance was balm to Hoyt's soul. Part of him hated Kofi for giving this to him.

"Count them out."

With that order, a stinging smack seared across Hoyt's backside. This was not like the spanking from before. Though that one had hurt, it had mostly turned him on. This was pure punishment. "One."

The second one landed on the other side of his ass, probably leaving a matching handprint.

"Two."

Kofi hadn't given him a total, so Hoyt couldn't anticipate the end. He counted higher as the spanking went on and on. His ass felt like it was on fire, and a sob escaped from somewhere deep inside. Full of unmet need and yearning, it was a sound of infinite sadness and abandoned hope. Somehow the spanking shook it loose and set it free, and with it came a kernel of peace that had been absent for so long, Hoyt had forgotten how to feel it.

A second sob followed, rendering him unable to continue counting. That's when Kofi stopped. "You're going to feel this for a few hours."

"Thanks." The sarcasm option on Hoyt's attitude had not been extinguished. If anything, the sense of peace had restored it.

Kofi chuckled. "You're welcome."

Hoyt hiked his shorts up to cover his nakedness, and he turned away from Kofi.

The alpha caught him by the shoulders and forced him to turn back. Hoyt kept his gaze pointed at the floor because he didn't trust himself not to lose the little composure he had left if he met Kofi's gaze.

"It's okay for you to be upset with me. It's okay for you to be angry. It's not okay for you to speak to me disrespectfully, call me names, or accuse me of things you know are untrue."

"You followed me here." Hoyt didn't just refer to Kofi coming into his apartment; he meant the move to Bear's Cove.

Kofi grasped his chin, forcing Hoyt to lift his gaze. Once he did, he found a wealth of patience and affection reflected in those deep blue depths. Hoyt didn't quite know what to make of it. Why wasn't Kofi irate?

The alpha held his gaze steady. "I did follow you here, and I'm not sorry."

Fueled by that admission, a bit of Hoyt's fire returned. He shoved Kofi's arms away, breaking his hold. "I'm going to make your life miserable. I'm not going to pay rent. It's going to take you years to evict me. And I'm going to bring home lots of men and have loud sex with the windows open."

For the first time, danger signs flashed. The neon glare nearly blinded Hoyt. From the fury darkening Kofi's skin to the way the alpha seemed to grow larger, Hoyt knew he'd gone too far.

Kofi leaned closer. His hand snaked out, but there was no violence in the movement. His palm rested low on Hoyt's abdomen. "Don't pay the rent. I prefer to be the one who provides for my omega and my child anyway. But make no mistake—as long as you're pregnant with my child, I'll disable any man who touches you."

Hoyt blinked. That had not gone in a direction he'd anticipated. "Pregnant? I'm not pregnant."

A chilling smile curled Kofi's lips. He snatched up the open beer Hoyt had yet to drink. Then he went to the refrigerator and took the rest of the pack. "We're ordering pizza and fruit salad tonight. You're welcome to join us." Then he held up the beer. "But you're not drinking these."

Kofi left. The door closed, and Hoyt sank down on the nearest chair. His bottom burned from the spanking, but he was too stunned to care. Pregnant? Was that why he'd been so moody lately?

His hand dropped to his abdomen. Bears gestated for around twenty weeks. If Kofi had impregnated him the last time they'd had sex, then that put him at four weeks. Was it possible? He'd never gone into heat when he was married to Dak. They'd thought that perhaps he was barren. It was one of the reasons Hoyt had filed for divorce. He hadn't wanted to remain in a loveless, sham of a marriage with no possibility of producing children.

Had he—unknowingly—experienced his first heat with Kofi?

He needed to see a doctor.

How was he going to open a coffee shop and manage a baby? Chase had a husband and a great-grandmother to help him out. Hoyt had nobody. His parents would help out, but only if he abandoned his dream and moved back to Forrest Hills.

He didn't know how long he sat there before a knock at the door drove all thoughts from his head. He stared at the beach-themed wreath hanging on the inside. His foot twitched, but that was all for movement on his part.

It opened, and Cruz stuck his head inside. "Hello? Hoyt?"

Words failed him. At least it wasn't Kofi. He wasn't sure he could deal with that alpha right now.

Cruz came inside, his gaze sweeping the room until it landed on Hoyt, and he smiled. "There you are. I brought pizza and fruit salad. Kofi was concerned that you don't have much food in your fridge."

He set the pizza box on the table in front of Hoyt, and he placed a bowl of diced melons next to it.

"Dak went home, and Ash and I thought maybe Kofi wouldn't be welcome just now, so I volunteered to bring you some food." Cruz opened and closed cupboards and drawers until he found plates and forks, which he brought to the table. He loaded pizza and fruit onto Hoyt's plate.

"You don't need to do this."

"There it is." Cruz flashed a smile to go with his teasing tone.

Hoyt stared at Cruz, wondering if the child he carried would resemble him or Kofi, or if it would favor the darker coloring that Cruz and Ashwin had inherited.

"And it's gone." Cruz stacked two slices of pizza on top of each other and took a bite. "I was thinking you'd want to talk."

Memories flashed through Hoyt's mind of the hours he'd spent with Cruz over the years. They'd never once had a negative interaction, not even when Hoyt had divorced Dak. None of the Freemans had been mean to him, but they'd all stopped communicating with him— not that he blamed them.

He picked at a cube of honeydew. "About what?"

Cruz shrugged. "Whatever. I haven't seen you in months, not since the funeral, and that was a crazy busy time, so we haven't had a chance to catch up in over a year. Tell me about your new business."

Hoyt didn't see why Cruz cared so much. "You were there today. You already know."

For several moments, Cruz stared across the table as he munched his dinner. "We used to be friends."

Hoyt disagreed. They'd once been family, bound by marriage to care for and look out for each other. He'd chosen birthday gifts for Cruz, and he'd made sure the cupboard was stocked with foods Cruz liked whenever he'd visited. They'd hung out for hours on end, talking about a vast array of topics. It had seemed like friendship, but it wasn't.

They'd lost that connection when he'd left Dak. It was nobody's fault; it was just the nature of the beast.

Rather than explain all that, Hoyt lifted a shoulder.

"Hoyt, don't shut me out."

With a sigh, Hoyt picked at a cube of cantaloupe. "We were friends when I was part of your family. Then I wasn't, and our friendship ended. I'm not looking to become part of your family again, so don't feel obligated to pretend friendship."

Unfazed by Hoyt's observation, Cruz finished chewing his pizza. "Whether you meant for it to happen or not, you are part of my family again." He grinned. "And this time, it's forever."

For ten whole minutes, Hoyt had forgotten about the baby growing inside him. He looked across the room, to a picture of his parents with him and his brother when they were little. For so long, he'd wanted that. It wasn't fair that his dream was coming true in such a tragic way. A cub deserved to have two parents.

"You need someone in your corner." Cruz gestured with a piece of honeydew on his fork. "You need someone who is one-hundred percent, completely on your side. Normally that would be your alpha, but since you're mad at Kofi, that rules him out."

It sure did. And because Chase was married to Dak, it ruled him out as well. There was nobody here he could talk to about this. Sure, he'd forged acquaintances, but there hadn't been time to cement a lifelong friendship.

"What about Gideon? You guys used to hang out all the time in Forrest Hills."

Hoyt missed some of the friends he'd left back in Forrest Hills. Because his cafe was opening the next morning, Hoyt didn't have time to drive out there, but he could call. Gideon had always been there when he'd needed a shoulder to cry on, and toward the end of his marriage, he'd needed a shoulder quite often.

"Yeah. Maybe."

Cruz reached across the table and set his hand on Hoyt's. "When you needed help, you called Kofi. In your heart, you know Ash and I love you like a brother, and we'll be here for you no matter what. Sure, things got a little awkward when you guys got divorced, but you knew if you needed anything, we'd come running—just like you'd do for any of us."

Hoyt snorted. "You'd come because you're decent bears. You'd do that for anyone."

Glancing away, Cruz curled his lip in shame. "I'm not the wonderful, selfless person you make me out to be. When you guys split up, I didn't do a great job of staying in touch with Dak either. When our fathers died, you were the only one who knew how to get in touch with him." He lifted his gaze to meet Hoyt's. "You're the one who inspires all of us to be better. We drifted apart after we lost you."

Not knowing how to respond, Hoyt stared at his empty plate. He didn't remember eating all that food, but it was gone, so he must have. It was true he'd been the one to make sure cards and gifts went out and regular phone calls were made. The alpha brothers had always been receptive to his efforts. He hadn't realized how much they'd come to rely on him.

Cruz got to his feet and rinsed his dish. On the way out, he hugged Hoyt. "Just think about it, okay? You have my number, and I'm staying with Kofi, so I'm not far away."

Chapter 8—Kofi

Moving into his first house was a lot of work—and almost none of his things were actually in the house yet, not that he had much. For the past few nights, he'd stayed up late washing walls and painting rooms. Having Ashwin and Cruz there was a blessing. Not only had it been far too long since he'd seen his brothers, but their help had been invaluable.

Kofi's ability to paint a wall would not go down in history as a great achievement. In fact, Ashwin took away his paint roller, and Cruz refused to let him near the brushes.

So he ripped out carpet to reveal wood floors badly in need of refinishing. It looked like someone had shifted repeatedly inside the house without regard for what a bear's nails could do to the polished wood.

He rose, stumbling out of his sleeping bag, at five-thirty.

"Are you going to make coffee?" Ashwin's sleepy voice followed him into the kitchen.

"I'm going to a place that sells coffee. I'll get it there." Kofi shoved a slice of leftover pizza in his mouth. It had been sitting out all night in a cardboard box. The congealed cheese was a hard, chewy mass, but he didn't care.

"You're going there to work." Ash noted. He came into the kitchen, eyes still mostly shut, and ran a hand through his thick mass of dark hair.

"For free," Kofi added. "Endless cups of java are the one perk I expect."

To expect more would be to court disaster. Hoyt hadn't asked for his help. Given the events of last night, he might be hostile to Kofi's presence. Kofi hoped not. He hoped Hoyt had taken the time to process some of what had happened, particularly the part where Kofi planned to be a permanent fixture in his life whether he wanted him there or not—and Kofi firmly believed Hoyt did want him there.

Plopping down on a folding step-ladder, Ash sighed. "Cruz wouldn't tell me anything about his conversation with Hoyt last night either."

When he'd returned the night before, Kofi had expected Cruz to relate every detail. Instead, Cruz had dug his heels in. "I made the mistake of letting my loyalty to Dak interfere with my friendship with

Hoyt the first time. I've learned my lesson. Anything Hoyt shares with me is between us. I'm rooting for you two to get together, especially since you've got a little one on the way, but if that doesn't happen, I want it to be clear that Hoyt is still part of my family."

The sentiment caused Kofi to choke up. He wanted Hoyt to have a reliable family network. Kofi knew that Hoyt's brother, Valerian, was twelve years younger and while he tried to be supportive, he was like any eighteen-year-old male or juvenile bear—capricious at the best of times. He meant well, and in a few years when his hormones calmed down, his head would be in place where he could be a decent friend again.

Hoyt needed to embrace the Freeman brothers and the network of support they offered. Even if he didn't marry Kofi, the child he carried guaranteed he was an integral part of Kofi's life now.

Finishing off his pizza slice, Kofi wiped the grease from his hands on a paper napkin. "I respect Cruz's decision, and I hope Hoyt gained some sense of peace from having Cruz there last night. Somehow, I doubt it. I've never come across a more stubborn, distrustful bear in my life."

"He's been hurt." Ashwin snagged the last slice of leftover pizza. "He's always been super sensitive. Now that he's alone, he doesn't have an alpha to rely on to even him out. Not to mention the pregnancy hormones. But you know all this, you said that last night."

Kofi had said a lot of things after finishing off the beer he'd taken from Hoyt as well as the six-pack Chase had sent over. He'd confessed that he'd fallen for Hoyt the first time he'd set eyes on the handsome ginger.

He shoved his car keys into his pocket.

Ashwin's eyes widened. "Whoa—you're not going looking like that."

"Like what?" Kofi looked down at what he was wearing. He looked good in jeans and a tee shirt, and it was all he'd brought to the house.

"You haven't shaved in at least three days, and you wore those pants yesterday. They have grease stains and paint splatters." Ash hitched his thumb over his shoulder. "Go change."

Without grumbling, Kofi put on a clean pair of pants, and Ashwin gave him a disposable razor for shaving. It wasn't a great shave, but it would do for now. Ash had been right—Kofi looked a million times better. But now he was late. He rushed out the door and sped the mile to Hoyt's cafe.

The omega had set his hours to cater to the morning rush. He opened at six in the morning—he was out of the way for the going-to-work crowd, but his location was perfect to catch the post-workout crowd—and he closed at one in the afternoon. Kofi liked that Hoyt's business model targeted a particular audience to begin with and allowed for growth as his customer base expanded.

He entered the cafe to find it full. Customers lingered in booths, eating breakfast parfaits and egg sandwiches, and the line at the counter was almost out the door.

Hoyt was the only person working there. His round, friendly face was lit with happiness. His lips moved as he greeted a customer. The customer's gruff expression and displeasure at having to wait disappeared as he caught a little of Hoyt's contagious joy. Kofi's heart beat faster. He wanted to wrap his arms around his omega and greet him with a kiss. He wanted to bury his face in Hoyt's neck and inhale his scent.

Shaking away those domestic thoughts, Kofi went behind the counter and tied an apron around his waist.

Hoyt glanced back, an almost-scowl pinching his features. "What are you doing?"

"Helping. It's been a while since I've worked behind a counter, but I think I remember the basics." Ignoring Hoyt's disapproval, he stepped up to the counter. "I can help whoever's next."

As he made lattes, Hoyt came up beside him. "Don't you have a house to paint?"

"It turns out I suck at painting. Everybody has their limits. Ashwin and Cruz have it covered, and Dak is supposed to go over and help later." Unable to resist a small display of affection, he squeezed Hoyt's shoulder. "Thanks for asking, sweetheart."

The next time Kofi found himself in a position where Hoyt could say anything personal, an hour had elapsed, and there was a lull in the flow of customers.

"I'm hearing a lot of positive feedback." Kofi tried for a constructive start to the conversation as he restocked cups and lids. "They especially love your parfait. That was a great idea. I've never had it before, but I'm looking forward to trying it."

Hoyt had been taking care of refilling the refrigerated items. He straightened up and regarded Kofi, his narrowed eyes showing off their pale blueness and cynicism. "Take one on your way out."

"I'm not leaving yet. You're about to have another rush. This place will be a madhouse until about nine, when it'll taper off from the morning rush."

Hoyt closed the refrigerator and straightened up the picked-over display case that had been filled with food an hour ago. Kofi brought out the last of the parfaits and egg sandwiches. Together, they arranged the case to look fuller than it was.

"You may run out of food." Kofi scratched at a spot on his chin. "Do you have ingredients to make more today? I can handle the counter if you want to start cooking."

Hoyt reached up and took Kofi's hand, which arrested Kofi's breathing and made his heart thunder in anticipation. But Hoyt only dropped it after it was away from Kofi's face. "You nicked yourself shaving, and now you've scratched it open. I have a first-aid kit in the back."

Kofi followed the omega into the back room, not because he felt the need for any kind of cream or salve, but because he wasn't going to turn down a chance for Hoyt to take care of him. Hoyt needed an alpha who would nurture his need to take care of his family, and Kofi needed an omega who wanted to do those things. More than that, he needed Hoyt.

He remained still while Hoyt dabbed his chin with a cotton ball soaked in peroxide. Their eyes met, and an unexpectedly tender moment passed between them.

Kofi knew not to push Hoyt right now. He was too vulnerable, and coming on too strong would only serve to reinforce his stubborn nature. So Kofi spoke softly. "You know what part we skipped?"

The hand smoothing antibiotic over the small cut shook ever so slightly. "Wiping down the dining room tables."

"Dating." Kofi caught Hoyt with the force of his somber gaze and held him with the strength of his sincerity. "We skipped the part where we spend time together and get to know one another. We assumed that we knew everything there was to know about each other because we've known each other for a decade."

Hoyt finished ministering to Kofi. He turned away to stow the first-aid kit, and words tumbled out. "Maybe you're right. Maybe we rushed into having a very brief affair, but it doesn't change anything. So what if you've changed your mind? What's to say you won't just change it back? Nothing. Yeah, you bought a house, but you've always been the kind of man who rushes into—and out of—adventure. This is just another in a long line of temporary layovers in your life. One day you'll wake up, and you'll be seized by wanderlust, and you'll be gone. I don't want that in my life. I'm the kind of bear who finds a home and stays put. We're just very different from each other. We always have been. That's why our fathers never considered matching us up. I'm a lot more like Dak than I am like you."

These things were true, and as painful as they were to hear, Kofi couldn't stop the grin from stretching his lips. Hoyt was talking to him again. What's more, he was rambling. This was a good sign.

He set his would-be omega straight on the main issue. "I told you I traveled because whenever I came home, it killed me to be around you and not be able to claim you as my own."

In lieu of a response, Hoyt closed the cupboard and headed for the door to the small storage room.

Kofi closed a paw over Hoyt's shoulder, halting his attempted departure. "I'm here to stay, and not just because you're having my child. I'm not going to give up on what I know is right. You were meant to be mine."

From his position behind Hoyt, Kofi couldn't see his face, but he could hear the harsh exhalation of breath, and he could smell the scent of Hoyt's bear as it emitted hormones designed to ensnare a desired alpha.

It gave him the courage to press a little. "One date. If you decide we're not right together after that, I'll stop pursuing you. I won't leave though, and you're stuck with me for a neighbor. Whether you accept me or not, I won't abandon my child."

Seconds of silence elapsed, each a sharp axe poised above Kofi's chest. Finally Hoyt looked over his shoulder. "One date. If it doesn't go well, then you'll leave me alone."

Kofi thought about Hoyt's schedule and how he'd just opened his business. He didn't want to wait too long, but he knew Hoyt had to be exhausted. The circles under his eyes hinted at a night of poor sleep. "Wednesday. I'll take you to dinner." That would give Hoyt a few days to adjust to all the changes in his life. It wasn't a lot of time, but it was enough for a beginning.

"Okay. Sure. One date. Why not?" Hoyt nodded, small movements that revealed his attempt to talk himself into it.

The fact that he wasn't jumping at the chance bothered Kofi a little, but he figured that at least Hoyt hadn't outright refused him—and that was progress. He helped Hoyt for a few hours longer, and then he went home to work on getting his house ready for habitation.

He was standing in the bedroom across the hall from the master, tapping his foot, when Dak came in. Dressed in his deputy uniform, he was without Chase or Ezra. He strolled over to the window overlooking the front lawn. "Care to share your thoughts?"

"I was wondering whether this should be the baby's room."

Dak went into the hallway. This house had four bedrooms upstairs, two in the back and two in the front. He pointed to the

69

bedroom next to the master. "I'd put the baby there, with the bathroom between you. That way, if you and Hoyt get loud while you're loving in the nighttime, you won't wake him or her up."

Between the master and the bedroom Dak indicated were the bathrooms—the private one for the master and the one that served the remaining bedrooms—and a walk-in closet. There would be plenty of buffer.

Dak indicated the room Kofi had just considered. "Put Hoyt there. He won't be far from the baby, and he'll be close to you."

He wanted Hoyt in his bedroom, not across the hall. He frowned. "That's not where I want him."

"I know." Dak clapped him on the shoulder. "But right now he's in an apartment above the garage. The easiest way to get him in here is to offer him a room of his own. It'll be easier to get him to forget to be stubborn if he's close to you. Then he's seeing you all the time, having to talk to you because you live in the same house. I used to rub his shoulders and make him a cup of hot chocolate. He melts in the face of affection and chocolate."

"Good to know." Kofi scrunched his nose. "Dak, I'm going to make a point to not do the things you did. They may have worked for you, and please don't take this the wrong way, but I don't want to remind him of you when he's with me. We resemble each other quite a bit, and we have a lot in common personality-wise, and I already worry that he's thinking of you when he's with me."

Dak snorted. "If anything, he was thinking of you when he was with me. He's called me by your name a few times. It was awkward."

All Kofi could think about was that he should have said something all those years ago. The regret ate at his soul. "Dak, if I had stood up in that cafe ten years ago and said I wanted Hoyt, would you have been upset?"

"I would have been livid." Dak didn't pause to think about his response, meaning he'd already considered the idea. "At the time, all I wanted was to get married and have a family. Even though I hadn't met him, I was committed to making it work." He closed his eyes, blocking out a heavy emotion, though it showed on his face. "I would have hated you, and it would have torn our family apart. Maybe we all made a wrong decision that day, but at the time, we all did what we thought was best. I have to believe that's all anybody can do."

Kofi was trying like hell to do what he thought best for Hoyt and for their relationship. He looked around at the home he'd purchased. It was meant to have the laughter of children ricocheting from the walls. He looked forward to repainting walls because kids had drawn all over them or scuffed them up with toys or sports equipment. He wanted to help his sons and daughters learn to write great essays. He wanted to teach them to shift in the bathtub so their fur could be washed.

There was so much potential happiness here, a gift card waiting to be redeemed if only Hoyt would open the fucking envelope.

With an exhaled breath, he closed his eyes. Patience was the way to win back Hoyt's trust. "I asked him out on a date, and he said yes. I was thinking of taking him to Grazie in Matunus Bay. They have great pasta."

Bears loved food. Their lives revolved around good meals, and nothing communicated affection better than an excellent meal.

"Good call." Dak chuckled. "I took Chase there when he was pregnant. He ate two dinners."

A dreamy sense of longing suffused Kofi's limbs, but this time it had a hopeful edge. He imagined sharing a dessert with Hoyt—feeding him a spoonful of ice cream, watching his pale eyes light with pleasure, licking away a stray crumb from his lip.

After dinner, he planned to take Hoyt to the boardwalk for a romantic stroll next to the sea. He wouldn't make a move or push his agenda. Hoyt needed to be wooed with a slow, steady hand.

Chapter 9—Hoyt

The mirror showed a moderately handsome redhead wearing a slate gray suit. It clung to his body in all the right places, highlighting his best attributes, like the shape of his biceps and the roundness of his ass. His hair had been cut the day before, so it lay perfectly in thick, short waves. His round face ended in a sharp chin, lending a bit of strength to otherwise gentle features.

Only his light blue eyes betrayed the nerves stretched so taut he battled waves of nausea roiling through his stomach. He hoped Kofi didn't take him someplace really nice because Hoyt wasn't sure he was going to be able to eat anything. It had been years since he'd been on a real date. If he didn't count the ones with Dak—and really, he shouldn't because they hadn't dated until they'd been engaged—then he hadn't been on a date since he was seventeen.

This was the first one that really mattered.

He checked his watch and smoothed his hair. "Showtime."

A knock sounded at the door the moment his hand closed around the knob. He opened it to find Kofi on the other side. Kofi also wore a suit. His was black like his midnight hair. Combined with that inviting smile and those eyes that seemed to see through him to discern his innermost thoughts, it made him look like a vortex of sin Hoyt wanted to jump into. Looking at this alpha liquefied Hoyt's bones. He fell back a step.

To cover it up, Hoyt lamely pointed to the stairs leading from his door down to the driveway. "I was going to come down."

Kofi's slow gaze swept up and down Hoyt's body, a sensual caress that calmed his nerves and stimulated his blood. He held up a single rose, which he pinned to Hoyt's lapel. "A gentleman always comes to the door. You deserve to be treated with respect. Expect nothing less."

Two minutes into the date, and already Kofi was giving orders. It warmed Hoyt's heart. As he locked up, he felt his body blooming from Kofi's nearness. The feeling continued as Kofi opened the car door for him.

Once they were underway, he ventured light conversation. "So, where are you taking me?"

Kofi glanced over, a playful lift to his lips. "Grazie. I heard it was amazing."

That was way over in Matunus Bay. "You heard? Haven't you eaten there?"

"No. This'll be my first time."

Hoyt kind of liked that there was no chance Kofi had taken another date to that restaurant. "What made you choose it?"

"They have excellent pasta, and I know how much you like pasta." He chuckled. "I remember that one Wardens Day when you made six different types of pasta salad. Every one of them was so good. I miss your cooking."

Was Kofi digging for an invitation to a home-cooked meal? Over the years, he'd never said much about the meals Hoyt had prepared, aside from a brief, positive review and gratitude. "You really like my cooking? It's not that great. I use recipes. I have a whole bunch of cookbooks, and I get even more ideas online. I don't make anything up myself. I'm not that creative. Those breakfast parfaits everyone liked so much came from one of my cookbooks. I'm literally layering vanilla yogurt, granola cereal, and fruit in a cup and people are buying it."

Amazement kept Hoyt's eyes wide as he thought about the brisk business he'd been doing for the past five days. He sold out of parfait before the morning rush ended every day. Word was spreading about his delicious creation, which was something he'd thrown together at the last minute.

All of these details—and a great deal more—poured out of his mouth in an avalanche of words. For the first time in his life, he didn't feel the need to hold back or censor his thoughts with Kofi. The alpha was here because he wanted get to know Hoyt better, and Hoyt's self-imposed gag order had been lifted.

Of course, it took him a while to remember his manners. The car rounded a curve, revealing the majesty of Matunus Bay, and he realized he'd been talking for the past three-quarters of an hour. Kofi had contributed encouraging noises and a few questions. Mostly he'd smiled as he listened.

"I'm hogging the conversation," Hoyt said. "Sorry. How was your day? Are you getting moved in okay?"

He'd noticed Kofi wasn't always at the house, and he didn't sleep there most nights.

"The rooms are all painted. I tore out the carpet. There's beautiful hardwood beneath them, so I'm having them refinished. A company was out today, and they should finish up tomorrow. I hadn't realized how large the house was."

Hoyt laughed. "Didn't you look at it before you bought it?"

"Yeah."

"And you saw how big it was? I mean, that house is massive. It's usually rented by a couple of families. It's a good location for vacationers—close to the beach and less than a mile walk from shops and such." He was doing it again—speaking without thinking. He fell silent.

"I noticed it was spacious, but the exact size didn't seem real until I had to wash down all those walls."

"I bet Ash and Cruz noticed how big it was since they painted it all."

Kofi's soft laugh washed over his nerves, a soothing balm. "Yes, they did."

"Cruz and Ashwin came by to see me this morning. They said they were heading back to the Rockies today."

"Dak and I took them to the airport this afternoon." Kofi's smile had an edge of sadness. "I loved that they came out. It was nice to spend time with them. I remember when we were cubs, we used to spend all day together, and then we'd have sleepovers in each other's rooms at night."

"They really like living in the Rockies. Ashwin told me bear culture is totally different out there, like it's common for an omega to have multiple alphas. And Cruz said sometimes omegas have their own omegas. Can you imagine?"

Kofi's mouth turned down in a brief frown, and then it vanished. "I don't have to imagine. Last summer, when I went out to stay with them for a few weeks, I was invited into one of those arrangements."

Fingers of jealousy squeezed Hoyt's chest, but curiosity won out. "Did you try it?"

"No. I'm a one-omega kind of bear. I don't want to share or be shared. That happens as well—that an alpha has multiple omegas."

"Oh." Hoyt couldn't imagine sharing an alpha with anyone. "I guess it's only fair that if an omega has more than one alpha, then an alpha can have more than one omega. How do they know who fathered which cubs?"

"I'm not sure they care. From what I've seen, when an omega has a cub, all of his alphas are considered the father. It's like the cub has three or more parents, which is actually kind of cool. There's always someone around to care for the cub." He parked the car and glanced over, his gaze roving meaningfully over Hoyt. "Of course, two parents can take care of a cub just fine."

Inside the restaurant, their table looked out over the bay. Though the view was spectacular, Hoyt found it increasingly difficult to tear his gaze from Kofi. He found himself lost in staring at Kofi's lips, the flat of his cheek, or the curve of his earlobe. They were small things, but this was the first time he felt like it was okay to study the alpha the way he'd always wanted.

Hoyt talked a lot, but Kofi didn't seem to mind. He listened, hanging on every word as if they all meant something. After dinner, which was fantastic, they walked on the path next to the water. Kofi took his hand, and joy rushed through Hoyt's system, not that this entire night hadn't been magical.

"I talk too much," Hoyt said. "You can tell me to stop, you know— before I get on your nerves."

Kofi glanced over, concern marring his brow. "I love to listen to you. I love that you say whatever's on your mind. Your voice is the sweetest music I've ever heard. I'm never going to tell you to stop."

At home, Kofi walked Hoyt up the stairs to his door. He waited while Hoyt unlocked it. "Do you want to come in?" Remembering the feel of Kofi's body against his, Hoyt hoped Kofi wanted to recreate some of that magic.

Kofi shook his head, his deep blue gaze roving Hoyt's features as if he was memorizing them. "You need to get to bed. I know how early you get up."

He moved closer. The omega swayed, a magnet caught in a field, toward the alpha. Kofi's lips brushed Hoyt's, a gentle affection communicating a wealth of feeling. "I want to see you again."

Hoyt had closed his eyes for the kiss. They popped open now. "I'd like that."

"Saturday?"

Why would Kofi want to wait so long? Neither of them worked evenings. "Tomorrow?"

"I have a deadline, and I've been busy this past week, so I'll need the next couple days to catch up on work."

He pictured Kofi bent over a laptop, typing away for hours on end. His caretaker instinct kicked in. "All that work isn't going to leave you with time to make a good meal. Are you still staying with Dak and Chase?"

"Yeah." Kofi chewed his lip. "Chase and Simone love to cook, so there's always something to eat. Don't worry about me."

He glanced over his shoulder, taking in the homey setup of his apartment. He didn't want to wait three days to spend time with Kofi again, but he understood Kofi's need for time to regroup. Hoyt knew he was a lot for people to take. "Oh. Okay. Saturday, then."

Kofi leaned in for another kiss. This one was deeper. Though he didn't wrap his arms around Hoyt, he still managed to make his body tingle with anticipation. When it ended, he stepped back. "I'll be there in the morning to help you in the shop."

"You don't have to."

"You hired someone?"

This was something he should have done before he opened for business, but he hadn't thought he'd be that busy. "I set up a couple of interviews for tomorrow afternoon."

"Good." Another bone-melting kiss followed. This time, Kofi's hands came to rest on his sides. "If you want to see me before Saturday, maybe you should invite me over for dinner. I wouldn't turn down one of those delicious pasties you make."

"Pasties?" Hoyt blinked. He'd never heard of pasties. "I think you have me confused with someone else."

Kofi brushed his thumb along Hoyt's lower lip. "I'd never confuse you with anyone else, sweetheart. My fathers loved them as well. They raved about those meat pies with rutabagas, carrots, and potatoes. I ate them a lot when I lived in Michigan one winter. They reminded me of you."

Relief flowed through Hoyt. "Pot pies. You want a pot pie. Okay, I can do that."

Another kiss. Hoyt didn't think he was going to be able to stay on his feet for much longer. Kofi's kiss made his whole body feel like jelly, a mass of need yearning for an alpha's touch. But after Kofi released him, he started down the stairs. "Lock the door, omega. I'm not moving into the house until Saturday."

The next morning, Hoyt was exhausted. Owning Perfect Blend was a dream come true, and he'd always been a morning person, but something seemed to be slowing him down. As he shoveled down cold cereal, he remembered that he was pregnant. Over the past few days, he'd ignored Kofi's assertion, but some things were becoming startlingly clear—like the bump that had popped out on his stomach overnight.

He mustered up energy to sail through the breakfast rush. Thank goodness Kofi showed up to help him every morning. There was no way he would have been able to handle it otherwise.

This location had turned out to be great for a number of reasons. Though it was a little out of the way, the easy parking, good coffee, and the breakfast parfaits made it worthwhile. Word of mouth had only increased traffic to his place. Now people were expressing an interest in having Perfect Blend open all day instead of only in the morning.

Hoyt wasn't ready for that, but he was pleased to know customers would welcome the expansion.

He slogged through the interviews. Among the two high-school students looking for summer work, the stay-at-home dad who couldn't come in until nine, and four others, nobody stood out. However, a couple of them seemed like they'd be fine. As he was cleaning up for the day and prepping for the next day's rush, the bell over the door chimed. He'd forgotten to lock it after the last applicant had left.

"We're closed."

"I drove all this way to try your coffee, and you're going to kick me out?"

Hoyt had turned as the customer started talking. A smile lit his face as he recognized Gideon. He hurried across the dining room to hug his friend. "I can't believe you came all this way. I thought you had to work?"

Gideon grinned, his eyes wide with excitement. "I am working. I got a promotion, which has landed me a larger and more lucrative sales route in Bear's Cove, Matunus Bay, and several smaller towns in the area. This morning, I met with three different doctor's offices." He motioned to the counter. "I was serious about that coffee. I need a boost."

Hoyt had begun cleaning the machines, so choices were limited. "I can brew you a cup of regular."

"Sounds fantastic." He set down an attaché case and threw his arms around Hoyt in a tight embrace. "I'm sorry it took me so long to get down here."

Hoyt had followed Cruz's advice to talk to someone who was firmly in his corner. He'd called Gideon, and just hearing the voice of someone whose friendship had outlasted his marriage helped. They'd talked about a myriad topics, though Hoyt hadn't brought up the one that it had taken him until this morning to admit was really happening.

He set a pot to brewing. "Congratulations on your promotion. Are you going to move to this area?"

"Not sure. Driving four hours one way is not my idea of an ideal way to spend a morning, but it's just a couple days each week. I can do the rest of my job from home. I was hoping to crash at your place tonight?" Gideon tucked his hand under his chin and fluttered his lashes prettily.

"It's small, but you're welcome to crash on my couch. It converts to a sleeper."

"Perfect. My day is packed with meetings, and I wasn't looking forward to driving back late tonight."

Gideon didn't stay long. As he'd said, his day was packed with meetings. Hoyt didn't get home until almost five. He sat down on the sofa to rest for a second, and the next thing he knew, the sharp rap of knuckles on wood roused him from a deep slumber.

Groggy, he dragged himself to the door and opened it. Kofi stood on the other side, a visual feast dressed in loose jeans and a form-fitting blue shirt that brought out his eyes.

It took a moment, but Hoyt remembered he'd agreed to bake pot pies. Also, he realized he hadn't showered or changed his clothes from the morning at Perfect Blend. He clapped a hand over his mouth. "I'm so sorry. I fell asleep."

Kofi's smile faded, replaced by concern. "Are you feeling okay?"

"Yeah. I'm just—I—Fuck. I'm sorry. I'm so sorry. I did those interviews, and then—"

Sliding past him into the apartment, Kofi pushed him back and closed the door. "Sweetheart, it's okay. Being pregnant takes a lot out of you. You're growing a brand new shifter cub from scratch. That's hard on a body." He pressed a kiss to Hoyt's cheek. "Go get changed, and I'll take you out."

"That's okay. I know you're trying to get work done. You should go back to Dak's. I'm sure Chase or Simone or someone cooked." Dak had always been good about sharing meal prep duties, and he was a decent cook.

"You come first. Let's get you fed, and then you can go to bed early tonight." Kofi's appraising gaze penetrated deep into Hoyt's mind. "Change of plans. Take a shower and get into your pajamas. I'll run out and grab something. Are you in the mood for anything specific?"

Tears leaked from Hoyt's eyes, and he wasn't sure why emotion choked his throat. Yes, he was an emotional person, but he didn't usually run around crying because someone offered to get takeout.

Before he could apologize, Kofi's arms were around him. Making soothing noises, the alpha led him to the sofa. Hoyt nestled into Kofi's embrace, burying his face in Kofi's chest until he got the eyeball leakage under control. The whole time, Kofi held him, stroking his hair and rubbing his back.

Hoyt sat up, sniffling, and reached for the tissues. "I'm sorry. I don't know what's wrong with me."

"Hormones," Kofi supplied. "You've always been sensitive, and now you're just more so." He grinned. "Are you ready for your shower?"

There were a lot of things Hoyt wasn't ready to do, like accept the fact that in three months, he'd have a cub to care for. Accepting other people and their baggage had never been a problem for Hoyt. He was the first one to offer help and the last one to leave. But he'd never been great at facing his own problems, be they physical, social, or emotional.

A shower, he could handle. "You don't need to stay. I know you have work to do."

Kofi didn't move from his place in the corner of the sofa. He rested an arm along the back of the cushion. "You are my priority, sweetheart. Work can wait. Right now, I'm going to take care of you because there's nothing I'd rather be doing."

"Those books don't write themselves." Hoyt bristled.

A wry smile twisted Kofi's luscious lips. "Look, I'm fine. I want to be here with you. Even if you were feeling fine, I'd have found an excuse to linger here with you. I'm trying to be patient, to give you time and space while we slow down and do this right, and that's why I offered to see you on Saturday instead of tonight. It's not because I don't want to see you—I do—it's because I don't want you to feel pressured. I want you to want to be with me."

Hoyt had always wanted to be with Kofi. Right now, things were good. Better than good—they were a dream come true. But he kept waiting to wake up and find out it was all a cruel dream—that Kofi wasn't actually his.

Because Kofi seemed to understand this, it made Hoyt fall for him even more. "Ribs. Or chicken parmesan. Something with protein."

As he suggested protein, a sultry thought occurred. He slid to his knees and crawled between Kofi's legs, his body in full flirt mode. Kofi sat back and regarded Hoyt thoughtfully. "Omega, what are you doing?"

Hoyt ran his palms up the inside of Kofi's powerful thighs and over the bulge at the apex. Then he went for the button.

Before he could undo it, Kofi's hand closed over his, halting his action. "I asked you a question. What do you think you're doing?"

He let a teasing smile play around his lips. "I'm craving protein." Since Kofi didn't have a tight hold on his hands, he undid the button and went for the zipper.

Kofi seized both hands and held them away from his body. "I just told you I wanted to take this slowly. Tonight I'm going to feed you dinner, and then I'll snuggle on the sofa with you until you're tired enough to fall asleep."

In shock, Hoyt blinked. He'd never heard of an alpha turning down a blowjob. Even when his marriage had been falling apart, his alpha hadn't refused this. Hell—no omega would turn it down either. "Are you one of those alphas who won't have sex with an omega if he's pregnant?"

"No." Kofi lifted him to his feet as he got up. "I'm one of those alphas who is so desperately in love with his omega that he cares more about not fucking up again than he does about getting his dick sucked on. We're not there yet, Hoyt. We're not to the point where you're ready to trust me to be your alpha." He traced a caress down the side of Hoyt's face. "You're worth the wait."

He followed up his heartfelt declaration with a deep kiss that left no doubt about the strength of his passion for Hoyt.

"I'll get ribs from that place on Sixth and Lone Pine." He nibbled another kiss on Hoyt's lips. "You take a shower and relax. I'll be back soon."

Chapter 10

Kofi

Patience was proving difficult, especially when Hoyt got that look on his face, the one that begged to please his alpha.

As Kofi waited in his car for the ribs to be brought out, he closed his eyes and wondered how long it would take for Hoyt to overcome the hurt he'd dealt to his omega. Would he be able to tell if Hoyt was ready for the next phase of their relationship? He'd never been in a serious relationship with a bear before.

A knock on the window interrupted his musings. A boy held up a carryout bag. Kofi unrolled his window. The boy handed it through. "Three orders of ribs, two orders of large mashed potatoes, six ears of corn, and one apple pie."

"Perfect. Thanks." He'd ordered extra of everything because Hoyt was eating for two. The leftovers might get him through the next day as well.

On his way up the steps to Hoyt's apartment, he gazed longingly at his empty house. Dak and Chase were helping him move his things in the next day, so he'd be closer to Hoyt. In some ways, it would be worse to be there, living and sleeping so close to his omega while not being close enough.

Hopefully it was only for a little while. He knocked on the door. If Hoyt was still in the shower, he could use his landlord's key, but he wanted to avoid that until he had explicit permission.

The door opened, and a strange man regarded him with a hint of curiosity. "Yes?"

The guy looked familiar. He was nearly as tall as Kofi, with broad shoulders and a strong build. It took a moment, but he recognized the visitor. This was the man who'd propositioned Hoyt at the omega's bonfire. Due to the man's size, Kofi hadn't been sure the man was actually an omega. He was larger than the typical omega, but he didn't quite have the air of an alpha.

Kofi looked the man up and down. "Gideon, right?"

The man's eyebrows both lifted. "Yes, that's right. Have we met? Wait—you're one of Dak's brothers. We have met a few times." He motioned behind him. "Hoyt is in the shower. Is he expecting you?"

He'd better be. Kofi put a leash on his jealousy and went inside, forcing Gideon out of his way. He didn't remember Gideon from anything except that night in the park, and he didn't look kindly on anyone who propositioned his omega. However if this man was an omega and he was one of Hoyt's friends, then Kofi needed to be nice. It was a good thing he'd picked up extra food.

"He's expecting me." He set the bag down on the table, and then he crossed the living room to knock on the bathroom door. "Hoyt, I'm back. Dinner is ready."

Gideon lingered near the door. "Am I interrupting something?"

Hoyt emerged from the bathroom in time to hear Gideon's question. "You're fine." To Kofi, he said, "Gideon is a pharmaceutical rep, and his new route brings him through Bear's Cove. I told him he could crash on the sofa tonight. It folds out."

First Kofi looked over Hoyt's clothing choice. He wore red plaid pajama pants and a gray cotton shirt. His feet were bare, and his hair was wet. Hoyt had followed orders, which soothed Kofi's alpha beast. Next he considered that if he wanted Hoyt to trust him, then he needed to extend his omega the same courtesy. Plus, some of the things Kofi adored about Hoyt were his generous spirit and his gregarious personality.

He opened cupboards in search of plates. "I brought lots of food, Gideon. I hope you like ribs."

"Love them." Gideon smacked his lips.

The trio sat down to dinner.

"Okay, let me get this straight," Gideon said as he ripped meat from the bone. "You two are together now?"

Kofi licked sauce from his fingers, his silence throwing the question to Hoyt. He was curious how the omega would characterize their relationship.

Hoyt watched him, an uncertain light to those sexy baby blues. "I'd say so."

A slow smile stretched Kofi's mouth, and a sense of satisfaction filled him. Though Hoyt was behaving as if he belonged to Kofi, he hadn't said the words before. It made a difference.

Gideon looked from Hoyt to Kofi. "Did you two have plans? I can go get a hotel room."

"You're fine," Kofi said. "I'll be heading to Dak's place after dinner. He's going to help me move some of my things into the house I recently purchased."

Hoyt's lips parted. "You're moving in tonight? You didn't tell me it was tonight. You said Saturday. I'll get dressed." He stood, but Kofi yanked him back down.

"Finish your dinner, and you won't be moving my things. Tomorrow, if you want, you can come by and help me unpack, but tonight you need your rest." He nailed Gideon with a firm look. "Hoyt is exhausted. Please don't keep him up tonight. I know you came a long way and you don't see each other as often as you did when he lived in Forrest Hills, but his health needs to come first."

"His health?" Gideon peered at Hoyt. "Are you sick?"

"Pregnant." Hoyt dropped that on the table as he scooped another helping of mashed potatoes onto his plate. "Kofi knocked me up."

That night, Kofi fell asleep, alone in the guest bedroom at his brother's house, wearing nothing but a big smile.

Hoyt—Three Weeks Later

The last of the morning rush subsided, and he was finally able to breathe. He leaned back against the counter and did exactly that.

"It seems like we get busier and busier every day." Lauren, the woman he'd finally settled on and hired, wiped down the sales counter before grabbing the bussing cart to clean the tables and booths. She was a few years older than Hoyt. She had a friendly face and a stout figure. He liked that she showed up on time, did her job without needing a lot of reminders, was pleasant to the customers, and didn't press or pester him with her opinion. They had lovely conversations.

"I keep waiting for it to drop off. This honeymoon period can't last forever." Somewhere in his head, Hoyt had been convinced this venture was doomed to failure, just like everything else he'd tried. His degree from college was in literature. He'd chosen it because he loved to discuss salient issues from all works, great and small. It was completely useless for helping him navigate the legal issues surrounding running a business.

"Sure it can." Kofi's voice preceded him from the back room.

Hoyt's mood brightened, and his flagging energy picked up. "I didn't see you come in."

"I know." He held out a small pastry box.

"You brought me a donut?" Hoyt clapped his hands together.

Kofi winced as he handed it over. "It's not a donut. Sorry." He nodded across the room. "Hi, Lauren. How are you?"

"Fine, thanks for asking. And you?"

"Fantastic."

Hoyt read the Sweet Treats logo on the top of the box and reflected that he needed to order cups and parfait containers with a Perfect Blend logo. It would help advertise his brand. He opened it up to find a single cupcake inside. To be fair, it was a huge cupcake, like it had swallowed two others and hadn't yet digested them. Across the top, it said, "Congratulations."

"What's this for?"

Kofi leaned on the counter next to him. "Exactly one month ago today, you opened those doors for the first time."

This was to celebrate the one-month anniversary of Perfect Blend being open. "Awww. That's sweet. You didn't have to do this."

"I'm proud of you, sweetheart. You've worked hard, and it's paying off. You need to celebrate the milestones."

Hoyt set aside the cupcake and tilted his face up for a kiss.

Kofi obliged.

Hoyt grabbed a clean knife and cut the cupcake into thirds. "Lauren, come over here and get some sugar. I definitely couldn't do this without you."

Abandoning her task, Lauren hurried over. "I never turn down chocolate."

They enjoyed the treat, and then Kofi said, "I have to get going. I have a signing down the coast."

"Will you be back tonight?" Over the past month, Kofi and Hoyt had been together every day, even if it was for just a few minutes.

Hoyt was concerned because Kofi hadn't tried for more than heavy petting when they made out. He understood that Kofi wanted to take it slow, but this seemed a bit extreme. After all, he was already pregnant. The bump in his stomach had grown to mark the second half of his pregnancy.

"About eight."

"Gideon is staying with me."

That was another thing. When Hoyt had left Forrest Hills, he'd told Gideon his couch was always open, and Gideon was taking advantage of it. One or two days each week, he showed up at Hoyt's door. It saved him a lot of money in hotel fees, but it was becoming a bit of an imposition.

"Oh. I'll leave you guys to whatever you have planned."

"Sure."

Hoyt had been hoping for a different offer.

Kofi pressed a kiss to his lips. "Text me when you're home for the night." He passed a hand over Hoyt's swollen abdomen. "Bye, baby."

When he was gone, Lauren brought the trolley full of dirty dishes to the kitchen. "He's a good one."

Hoyt had been contemplating ways to tell Gideon both of them would be happier if one of them slept in a hotel every other week. "Who is?"

"Kofi."

"Oh, yes. I know."

Lauren gestured to his midsection. "Are you ever going to accept his proposal?"

His mind hadn't wandered, and yet he felt as if he'd lost the thread of the conversation. "Whose proposal?"

"Kofi's."

"He hasn't proposed."

She frowned. "He seems like the kind of man who proposes. I'm not usually wrong about people. That's odd."

"Oh—no, you're right. He is the kind of man who proposes. We—um—we had a miscommunication when we were first together, and we're taking our time coming back from that." Hoyt wondered how long Kofi wanted to wait. The anger and hurt he'd felt so strongly only five weeks ago had evaporated. It no longer mattered. Now he started every day looking forward to seeing his alpha.

"Seems like you've come back." Lauren finished loading the dishwasher and set it to running. As she gathered her things to leave for the day, she paused. "I may be out of line here, but it seems to me that you two are stuck in a holding pattern. If neither of you moves forward, then it's going to hold until it breaks. I'd hate for that to happen. You're so good together."

She patted his arm and left.

That evening, Hoyt packed an overnight case. When Gideon showed up, he had dinner with his friend, and then they hung out, chatting.

"I'm not going to be here tonight." Hoyt dropped his news casually into the conversation.

Gideon glanced over. "Please say you and Kofi have finally decided you're over this stupid timeout from your games of Hide the Sausage. I mean, you're already pregnant. You should be picking out furniture for the baby's room and arguing over names between bouts of frantic, hormone-fueled sex."

That about summed up where he hoped this was headed. Hoyt pointed toward Kofi's house. "If you need anything, I'll be there."

A huge smile split Gideon's face. "Awesome. When can we discuss me subletting this apartment from you?"

"Not yet." Hoyt wasn't completely sure how Kofi would respond. "Soon—hopefully."

Then he went to Kofi's house. It was locked, but he had a key for emergencies. They were neighbors, after all.

He set his bag down inside Kofi's bedroom and looked around. The entire house was beyond minimalist. After Ashwin and Cruz had painted it and Kofi had the floors redone, he'd moved in with all his furniture.

There wasn't enough furniture to fill up a quarter of the house. He had one sofa and one television for two living rooms. He had nothing in the dining room or the family room. His books and things had taken over the office, which was the most lived-in room in the entire place. Upstairs, the master bedroom had a bed and dresser, and the master bathroom held Kofi's hygiene items. The main bathroom had a roll of toilet paper sitting on the counter, and that was all—no soap or hand towels. The shower had no curtain. The bathroom on the main floor at least had soap and a towel that needed to be changed out.

With a huff, he shook his head. Kofi was definitely used to living alone in a small apartment. If Hoyt lived there, he would start with the bedroom and kitchen, and then he'd take on the bathrooms, both living rooms, and everything else.

But this wasn't his house yet.

He was banking on the "yet."

He pushed the panel on his pregnancy jeans down to rest under his belly, and then he made hot chocolate and settled on the sofa in front of the television. The rear entryway led to the hall dividing the family room from the kitchen. This was the main door Kofi used to enter and exit the house. Hoyt liked to think he'd developed this habit because he liked to check on Hoyt from a distance.

"Hello?"

"In here." Even though the sun had not yet set, evening shadows had cast much of the house in darkness. Hoyt had left on most of the lights. It was a large house, and he didn't feel comfortable enough to let the dark spaces persist.

Kofi appeared in the wide entryway, a surprised smile on his face. "I thought you were with Gideon tonight."

Hoyt went for brutal honesty, just as Lauren had advised. "I missed you."

The alpha came into the room and sat on the sofa next to him. He reached out and, resting his hand on Hoyt's shoulder, brushed the pad of his thumb across the omega's collar bone. "I've missed you too."

"I want to sleep with you tonight." Bald-faced truths were what they needed to catapult them from this holding pattern and onto higher ground.

"Okay, sure." Kofi eased his hand back as if physical contact was forbidden and he'd been caught breaking the rules. "Whatever you need."

"I need you to kiss me."

Faster than Hoyt could finish the last two words, Kofi closed the distance. His lips captured Hoyt's, and his tongue demanded entrance, taking its due once inside. He pulled Hoyt onto his lap, and his hands roamed the safe spaces—thighs, sides, and shoulders—taking a slower path toward stoking Hoyt's passions.

But Hoyt's passions had been simmering for far too long, and even the rolling boil had reached the limit on what it could safely handle. He shifted until he straddled Kofi's lap. Reaching between them, he undid the buttons on Kofi's shirt. As soon as he exposed flesh, he ripped his lips from Kofi's and kissed a path down his alpha's neck.

Kofi moaned, and his fingers burrowed into Hoyt's hair. His grip tightened until the pressure pulled Hoyt away from his task.

Hoyt sat back, his chest heaving from excitement and exertion. "What? Did I do something you don't like?"

"It's not that." Kofi closed his eyes, waging an obvious battle between desire and control.

Control won.

He got up, lifting Hoyt, and he set Hoyt on his feet. "It's been a long day. Let's get ready for bed."

Hoyt may have lost the first skirmish, but this wasn't over. He held Kofi's hand as the alpha went around checking that the house was locked up tight. Then he followed his alpha up the stairs.

Kofi disappeared into the bathroom. Hoyt heard the shower running. He debated surprising Kofi in the shower, but then he decided that he wanted him to surrender to passion. It would be too easy for his omega to goad Kofi's alpha into overriding the boundaries Kofi set in place. That's how he'd ended up pregnant in the first place.

He snagged a towel from the nearly bare linen closet and went into the other bathroom to brush his teeth and wash his face. This was not going as planned.

When he returned, he found Kofi already under the covers. He wore a full set of long-sleeved pajamas. Hoyt stripped out of his shirt and pregnancy pants—which were the opposite of sexy—and got into bed wearing only boxers. He'd found a brand with a waist that stayed below his belly because it bothered him to have anything across it.

Kofi kept his eyes averted. His gaze didn't waver from their laser focus on the magazine in his hands.

Hoyt settled onto his pillow, folding his hands under his head. "I guess I hadn't realized how turned off you are by the changes to my body."

Kofi froze, not that he'd been moving before. "Quite the opposite, actually."

Snorting, Hoyt turned his back to Kofi. "All evidence points to the contrary."

"What evidence is that?" Kofi's breath whispered across Hoyt's bare shoulder.

He rolled to his back with the intention of giving Kofi a piece of his mind, but he found his alphas lips on his. This kiss was different from before, wild and insistent. The length of Kofi's body pressed alongside his, and he felt incontrovertible evidence supporting Kofi's claim.

The alpha was hard as a rock. Kofi's hips moved, thrusting his erection against Hoyt's thigh. Kofi broke the kiss, violently pulling away but his hips didn't stop. "Does this feel like I don't find you attractive?"

Hoyt cupped Kofi's cock through his pajama bottoms, stroking his length. "What's this?" He slipped his hand down Kofi's pants and stroked it without barriers. "It's soft, and yet it's hard. I can hold it in the palm of my hand, and yet it seems so big."

"Sweetheart, are you sure you're ready for this?"

He set his free hand on Kofi's cheek. "More than ready. I want to feel you inside me so badly it hurts. Please—take me, claim me, make me yours."

Kofi closed his eyes and breathed harder. "I want to make love to you."

Hoyt's finger pressed to Kofi's lip, halting any qualification he tried to add. "Then let's do, okay?"

Kofi took Hoyt's hand in his and lifted it to his mouth. He kissed a fingertip before sliding it into his mouth. The light scratch of Kofi's teeth sent a hundred tingles radiating up Hoyt's arm.

"I want to spank your luscious ass." Kofi moved his oral ministrations to the next finger. "I want to bind your wrists."

Hoyt was in favor of anything Kofi wanted to do to him. He especially liked what Kofi was doing to his fingers.

"I want to blindfold you."

"Yes," Hoyt gasped.

"I want to torture your balls until you orgasm."

"Yes, Daddy, yes."

With a terrific groan, Kofi captured his lips for another searing kiss, and then he stared into Hoyt's eyes. "I love you so much, sweetheart."

Hoyt's heart swelled. Kofi had said the words before, but this time seemed different. Something in Hoyt broke, and he recognized the last rope holding his distrust in place. For the first time, he truly believed Kofi meant everything he said. He smiled at his alpha. "I love you, too."

"Mmmm—use my title. I like it."

"Daddy?" He grinned. "I knew it would grow on you."

Kofi sprang from bed and went to his dresser. He rummaged in a drawer and came back with leather cuffs. "I don't have the patience to bind you with rope, so these will have to do. Hold out your wrists."

Hoyt watched as Kofi secured cuffs to each of his wrists. "Lie down."

Kofi tied him to the slats in the headboard by attaching the cuffs together with a short piece of leather. Now he was bound with his hands overhead. The covers ripped away, and he helped Kofi ease his underwear down his legs.

When he was naked and bound, Kofi stepped back for an unobstructed view. He undressed slowly, teasing Hoyt with the visual. Then he stroked his cock while his gaze roamed Hoyt's body.

"You are so fucking hot, omega. And you're mine, completely mine." The low timbre of Kofi's voice washed over him as Kofi's hand moved to a fevered frenzy. In no time, he grunted his release. His ejaculate spilled from his cock, spurting and splashing over the mound of Hoyt's belly.

Sated, Kofi regarded him with a soft smile. Then he went back to his dresser. This time, he returned with a sleeping mask, which he slipped over Hoyt's eyes. Blinded, Hoyt waited for Kofi's touch.

It came quickly. Kofi tied a leather strap around Hoyt's semi-hard cock and balls, which made it harder for Hoyt to achieve orgasm. Kofi's mouth closed around his dick, and his cock finished lengthening to a full erection. It hurt a little, but the pain subverted to pleasure quickly.

Wet and hot, Kofi's mouth and tongue wreaked havoc on his senses. He found himself unable to control his movements. His body jerked and twitched, and his hips thrust to the rhythm Kofi set.

"Yes. Fuck, yes, Daddy. Oh, that feels so unbelievably good."

Kofi added an element, pulling down on Hoyt's balls as he sucked. Agony turned to ecstasy, but orgasm remained elusive. Just when he thought he could stand it no longer, he found himself lifted and turned. The links between the cuffs clinked as they twisted together.

"Prop yourself up on your elbows and knees. There you go. Good job, sweetheart." Kofi caressed Hoyt's bare ass. "I've missed this ass more than you can possibly imagine. I've dreamed about spanking it and fucking it. The last time I spanked you, it was hard not to take some time to pay homage to this magnificent flesh."

Light kisses and strokes feathered across Hoyt's hindquarters, and then teeth sank into the naked flesh. Hoyt struggled to remain still as Kofi exercised his dominance by marking him in yet another place. Whimpers from his bear filled the room, and that only fueled Kofi. He finished the bite, and then his hand rubbed circles over the mark.

Hoyt's whimpering grew quieter, changing to a tone that begged for more.

With a volley of spanks, Kofi delivered. His hand rained blows over Hoyt's backside, heating his skin and reminding him how much he missed the feel of Kofi's firm hand meeting his flesh.

"Yes, Daddy, yes. Harder. Please don't stop."

A hand closed around his cock, spreading lubricant. It masturbated him while the other hand slowed the spanking. Occasional and irregular blows caught him unaware, heightening the pleasure spiking through his system.

He was close, so very close. If only Kofi hadn't tied his cock, he'd have come five times over by now.

The bed dipped as Kofi positioned himself between Hoyt's legs. He felt fingers spreading lube on his sphincter and reaching inside to fully prepare him. Then the head of Kofi's wide cock nudged his entrance. He exhaled as his alpha surged forward.

"You're mine, omega. I own you—heart, mind, and body."

"Yes," he breathed. "I belong to you, Daddy—heart, mind, and body."

With that Kofi made love to him. He thrust gently, with reverent touches that were in direct opposition to the violence of the foreplay.

After a time, Kofi guided Hoyt onto his back and removed the sleep mask.

Hoyt opened his eyes to behold his alpha, the only man he'd ever truly loved. He widened his legs, bringing his knees up, and Kofi fed his cock into Hoyt's body.

Kofi leaned over him, holding his weight on his elbows, and moved in him. Searing kisses punctuated this tender act. Hoyt relaxed, surrendering to Kofi's loving mastery.

Unhurried passion grew, and unexpectedly deep emotions detonated in Hoyt's core. Kofi freed his arms, and Hoyt ran his hands over every part of his alpha he could reach.

"Touch yourself," Kofi breathed. "I want to see you come."

Propping himself on one elbow, Kofi guided Hoyt's hand to his cock. Together, they stroked Hoyt to the point of frenzy. Something sharp broke inside him, and a sweet pain accompanied the intense pleasure rioting through his system. He cried out, a long, guttural cry that came from his bear as much as it came from his human side. Vaguely he was aware of Kofi's shout as he climaxed.

He lost all sense of himself as he floated on a sea of bliss.

When he came back, he found himself in Kofi's arms. The alpha had removed the cuffs and cleaned them both up, and then he'd curled his body around Hoyt's.

Hoyt pressed a kiss to his sleeping alpha's chest. "I love you, Kofi Freeman."

Kofi's eyes opened, and he regarded Hoyt with a sleepy smile. "I love you too, Hoyt, soon-to-be Freeman."

Hoyt had changed his name back to Graziano because the other name hadn't sounded right. This time, it did. He closed his eyes and fell asleep in his lover's arms.

Epilogue--Hoyt

"Welcome to Perfect Blend's first ever speed-dating, matchmaking event!" Hoyt's voice boomed through the speakers, and his announcement was greeted by whistles and cheers.

While he explained the rules to the patrons, his gaze kept wandering to the dark-haired alpha leaning against the window next to the front door. His arms were crossed, but his shoulders were relaxed, and his smile was directed at Hoyt. Though they'd only been together—sexually—for a few days, they'd already set a date for the wedding.

Kofi had moved Hoyt's things into his house. Tomorrow Hoyt planned to close the shop for the morning and go furniture shopping with Kofi. It turned out Kofi had purposely put off decorating until Hoyt moved in. They were building a life together, from the ground up.

The bell dinged, and the buzz of people talking filled the air. Hoyt made his way to his alpha who opened his arms in welcome. Hoyt pressed his lips to Kofi's.

"I like Perfect Blend better than Growl-N-Grind." Kofi chuckled.

Hoyt barely remembered his first choice for naming this place. He ground his pelvis against Kofi's, which was a feat because his belly was in the way. "Are you sure about that?"

"Omega, keep that up, and nobody is going to be running this event because I'll have you in the back room bent over a counter faster than you can get a word out."

"Wow." Hoyt grinned. "That's fast." He settled down and snuggled his cheek against Kofi's chest.

"I'm proud of you."

"Because I'm behaving?" Regular spankings went a long way toward quelling Hoyt's urges to be contrary. He looked forward to them, not only because he enjoyed them, but because if he was good, Kofi always made love to him afterward.

"No. I mean—yes, that—but no, I'm proud because you have a great place here. People like your coffee and they love you. I've heard people raving about this place all over town. You worked hard. You didn't let anything stand in your way. And here you are—the proud owner of a successful coffee shop."

Hoyt tilted his face up and batted his lashes. "And I finally landed the alpha I've wanted for so very long."

"Is this the part where I remind you that you would have had me sooner if you weren't so proud and stubborn?"

With a flagrant grin, Hoyt shook his head. "This is the part where I remind you that you find those qualities endearing and frequently sexually stimulating."

Kofi's hand played a caress up and down Hoyt's spine. "Good point. Hey—I had this idea for a sex scene in my next novel that I'd be able to visualize if we acted it out first."

Hoyt snorted, but the buzzer went off before he could respond. He bounced back to his microphone to move the speed-daters to their next table. From his spot near the door, Kofi winked and mouthed, "I love you."

That simple gesture of affection held a promise that warmed Hoyt's heart. He was finally in a coffee house with the right alpha.

He mouthed back, "I love you, too."

About A. J. Stone

A.J. Stone loves rainbows and bears. Follow A.J. on Facebook at https://www.facebook.com/AJStoneBearsCove/ or at www.michelezurloauthor.com to keep up with the newest releases, and feel free to request stories for your favorite Bear's Cove characters.

Reviews let A.J. know you want more!

Bear's Cove Series (MM/MPreg) by A. J. Stone

Dak's Omega
Tanzil's Second Chance
Perfect Blend: Kofi's Omega

Draco International Series (MM/MPreg) by A. J. Stone

Amaricio's Omega Shifter
Koren's Omega Neighbor
Zeke's Reluctant Omega

MM Romance by Nicoline Tiernan

Nexus #1: Tristan's Lover by Nicoline Tiernan
Nexus #2: The Man of His Dreams by Nicoline Tiernan

Sneak Peek at Amaricio's Omega

"You'll do fine, Edgar. Don't stress yourself out to the point where you throw up." On the other end of the line, Brielle sighed.

Edgar's younger sister and best friend was his rock and his cheerleader, but at times like this, he wished she wouldn't mention vomiting. It made his stomach churn. "Brielle, don't say the T-U word."

With his phone pressed to his ear, he bolted to the nearest bathroom. Then he rethought that strategy. The last thing he needed was the lobby full of potential candidates for the job and any other staff to hear him retching. He burst out of there and found an out-of-the-way restroom.

"Edgar, don't you dare do it." Brielle spoke firmly. "Breath. Inhale through your nose. Exhale through your mouth. You're good enough. You're smart enough. You earned this interview."

As if she had magic powers, her assurances made the sick feeling go away. "I wish you were hiring me."

"When I'm a famous singer, you can be my assistant, I promise. Hey—why don't you look at this like practice for taking care of me when I become a diva?"

He laughed. Brielle was the farthest thing from a diva he'd ever met. She volunteered every week to lead sing-alongs in retirement homes, and she fostered homeless dogs. If anything, she was too humble. Later that day, she planned to take the dogs she was fostering to an adoption picnic. They'd made special dog treats the night before to mark the occasion.

A notification sounded on his phone. "That's me. It's almost time for my interview. I'm going to wash my hands and get back to the lobby where I'll be lost in a sea of men and women wearing suits and vying for the same job."

"Luck and love," Brielle said, using their shorthand for *Best of luck* and *I love you*. "Call me after."

"Luck and love to you too. I will. Bye."

He slid the phone into his bag, and then he looked around, careful to keep his gaze away from the urinals where several men did their business. The restroom was clean. It had pale tan tile on the walls with ocher accents, and stacks of paper hand towels were near each soap dispenser. The public bathroom in this building was nicer than anyplace he'd ever lived. There was no way he was getting this job.

First off, he didn't have a suit. The nicest interview outfit he'd managed to put together consisted of khaki pants and a white dress shirt. He didn't even own a tie. He looked down at his brown dress shoes. Though they were shiny and well-kept, they'd seen better days. He looked good, but in no way did he look the part of personal assistant to Amaricio Granger, CFO of Draco International.

He wasn't sure what a CFO did or what Draco International sold, but he figured that a personal assistant did things like schedule dentist appointments and walk the dog. He could do that and stay out of the business end of things. Of course, everyone in the lobby waiting for their turn at an interview had a different interpretation of what the job duties meant. In all likelihood, they were right and he was wrong.

With a sigh, he surrendered to the inevitable disappointment. The interview would be good experience for his next one. He'd ask for feedback about what he could do better. People liked to do those types of things.

He used the facilities, and then he washed his hands.

A man came up next to him, talking on the phone in an unfamiliar language. His voice came out in a low rumble that Edgar felt more than heard, and he had a cologne that piqued Edgar's curiosity. Much like the others in the lobby, he wore a suit and tie. He had a rugged face with sharp features and strong lines. His dark hair and eyes added a sort-of mystique that made him handsome instead of unfortunate-looking. He had a distinguished air about him, an authority Edgar would want in a personal assistant. This guy got things done.

He ended the call and dried his hands.

As he turned away, Edgar noticed a crumb on the man's cheek.

"Hey, you have—"

The guy swiveled back, one brow raised.

Edgar lifted a hand to his own cheek to indicate the location of the crumb. "Blueberry crumble?"

He wiped at his cheek, missing the crumb. Instead of using the mirror to check, his gaze concentrated on Edgar. "Better?"

Edgar brushed it away, noting the smoothness of the man's skin. "The bakery down the street has the best blueberry crumble muffins. When I'm being very bad, I get one."

"Bad?" The accompanying frown was downright menacing.

Keeping a friendly smile because he realized the man had misunderstood his intention, he explained. "They have like a thousand calories. I swear, I eat one, and a love handle pops out to wave at me."

The man's sinful gaze wandered up and down Edgar's body, and then he seemed to dismiss it entirely. Okay, maybe the sinful part had been only in Edgar's mind. He sucked on the left side of his lower lip, a nervous habit Brielle said was endearing but probably wasn't all that great. His gaze fell to the man's tie.

It was a power tie, deep red with flecks of gold thread. "Oh, that blueberry sure gets away from you."

The guy's gaze dropped to the tie, and his growl matched his expression.

"I have a stain stick." Edgar opened the leather messenger bag he'd picked up at a charity resale shop for five dollars. A short rummage brought him to his prize. He held it up. "Here."

The frown was gone, but the quizzical look was back.

"It works. I swear. I just used it on my shirt this morning." He untucked a corner where he'd spilled coffee and lifted it to so the rugged man could see. "Coffee stain, gone. It's like magic."

Rugged man took it and dabbed at the stain until it disappeared. Then he handed the stain stick back. "Thanks."

"If this restroom had air dryers, you could dry your tie." He secured the lid on the stain stick and tucked it back into his bag. "Hopefully it'll dry before your interview."

"Interview?"

Edgar held out his hand. "I'm Edgar. Good luck today."

That confused look was back. "You're here to interview for the personal assistant job?" The guy shook his hand, but he made it seem like it was his idea.

The question made him self-conscious. He didn't know anything about the man or the company, and he hadn't thought it was the kind of job that required a suit. "Yeah. Snowball's chance for me, but maybe I'll treat myself to a blueberry crumble after."

The confusion morphed back into a frown. Rugged man came by that face honestly. "Why would you think you don't have a chance?" A gleam in his dark eyes demanded answers, and Edgar found himself giving them.

"No experience, and I don't own a suit. I was thinking this would be the kind of job where I picked up the dry cleaning, walked the dog, and went on coffee runs. Maybe do some emergency grocery shopping. I don't know—stuff a busy guy doesn't have time to do." He motioned in the direction of the lobby and leaned forward. "Those people all have business degrees. I don't know the first thing about business."

"But you're still going through with the interview?"

Edgar shrugged. "It'll be a learning experience."

The light in the man's eyes changed to thoughtful. His gaze wandered up and down Edgar again, this time with an appraising light.

"You helped me out even though you think we're competing for the same job."

"It doesn't hurt to be kind, and you're the one who has to live with yourself when you aren't." He tilted his head in a farewell to the strangely handsome stranger, and he returned to the lobby to wait for his interview.

He made it just in time.

A petite woman with black hair tied up in a neat bun commanded the space. "Everyone who has an eight-forty appointment, follow me."

Edgar and nine other people scrambled after her. She led them into a conference room.

"Have a seat."

The crowd scrambled for the seats as if the last one standing was going to be eaten by a shark. One woman even pulled a chair out from under a man. Not one to be pushy, Edgar waited for the others to sort themselves out. They did, and that's when he realized there were nine chairs.

The petite woman crooked a finger at him. He went to the front of the room. "Thank you for coming," she said. "You can go now."

The chair thing had been a test, and he'd failed. Though he'd known the job was a longshot, he still felt a bit of a letdown. He offered his hand. "Thank you, and you have a great day."

Surprise flitted across her features as she shook his hand. Her mouth opened like she was searching for something to say, but the door opened before anything came out.

Rugged man stepped inside. His gaze zeroed in on Edgar, and he pointed. "Him."

The lady with the tight bun seemed to find her voice. "You're sure?"

The frown he directed at her was nothing like the ones Edgar had seen in the restroom. This one answered the lady's question while simultaneously taking her to task for asking it. He left, closing the door behind him.

Edgar made to leave, but she stopped him. "Oh, no. You can't leave now. You got the job."

He motioned to the closed door. "That's what that meant?"

"Yes." Her smile softened. "Congratulations. You're now Mr. Amaricio Granger's personal assistant."